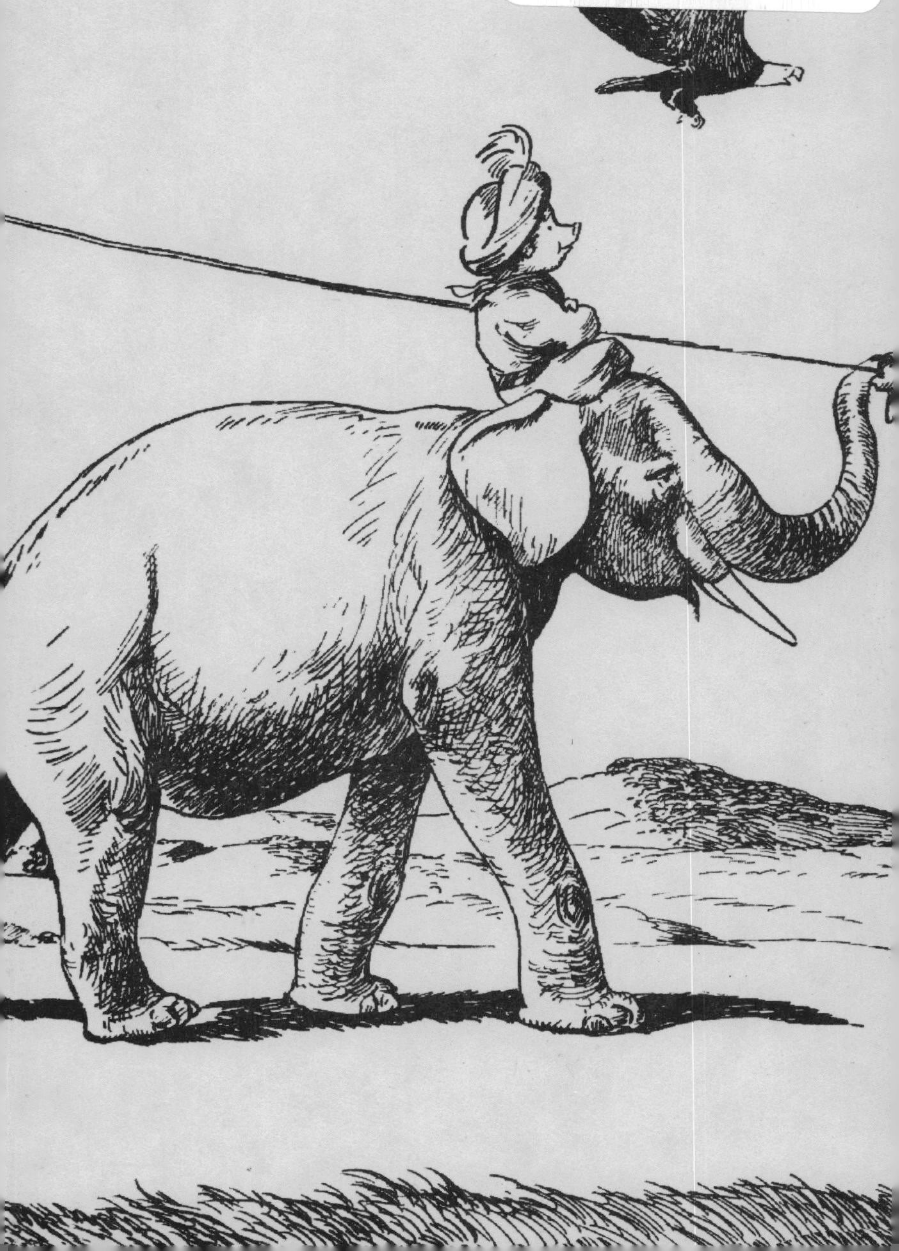

The Complete FREDDY THE PIG Series
Available or Coming Soon from the Overlook Press

FREDDY *and the*

PERILOUS ADVENTURE

". . . I'll bring everything back tomorrow."

FREDDY
and the
PERILOUS
ADVENTURE

by WALTER R. BROOKS

THE OVERLOOK PRESS
WOODSTOCK & NEW YORK

If you enjoyed this book, very likely you will be interested not only in the other Freddy books published in this series, but also in joining the *Friends of Freddy,* an organization of Freddy devotees.

We will be pleased to hear from any reader about our "Freddy" publishing program. You can easily contact us by logging on the either THE OVERLOOK PRESS website, or the Freddy website.

The website addresses are as follows:
THE OVERLOOK PRESS:
www.overlookpress.com

FREDDY:
www.friendsoffreddy.org

We look forward to hearing from you soon.

First published in the United States in 2001 by
The Overlook Press, Peter Mayer Publishers, Inc.
Woodstock & New York

WOODSTOCK:
One Overlook Drive
Woodstock, NY 12498
www.overlookpress.com
[for individual orders, bulk and special sales, contact our Woodstock office]

NEW YORK:
141 Wooster Street
New York, NY 10012

Library of Congress Cataloging-in-Publication Data

Brooks, Walter R., 1886-1958.
Freddy and the perilous adventure / Walter R. Brooks ; illustrated by Kurt Wiese.
p. cm.
Summary: A ballooning mishap sends Freddy the pig and some animal friends on a cross-country chase, on the trail of a blackmailing scheme, and into the prizefight ring.
1. Pigs—Fiction. 2. Domestic animals—Fiction. 3. Balloon ascensions—Fiction. 4. Adventure and adventurers—Fiction.] I. Wiese, Kurt, 1887- ill. II. Title.
PZ7.B7994 Fr 2001 [Fic]—dc21 2001033965

Manufactured in the United States of America
ISBN 1-58567-178-9
1 3 5 7 9 8 6 4 2

FREDDY *and the*

PERILOUS ADVENTURE

Chapter 1

Alice and Emma, the two ducks, sat on the bank and watched the breeze crinkle the surface of the duck pond into a sort of blue and silver carpet. The pond was the ducks' home, and they were just as proud of it as Mrs. Bean, down at the farm, was of her front parlor, with the new wallpaper and the picture of Washington Crossing the Delaware.

"Sometimes I think," said Emma thoughtfully, "that this is the most beautiful spot in the whole world."

"It's pretty enough," said Alice. "But as to its being the most beautiful spot in the world, how do we know? We've never seen anything of the world. Except for that trip to Florida we've hardly ever been off the Bean farm."

"Why, sister!" exclaimed Emma. "I — I thought you loved it here as much as I do. I thought we'd been very happy—"

"So we have," interrupted Alice. "So we have. But you must admit that there isn't anything very *new* about it. We swim round and round on the same water, and we dive into the same mud, and we see the same animals and hear them say the same things, day after day, week after week, month—"

"—after month," said a pleasant voice behind them, and they turned to see Freddy, the pig, who had come up unnoticed.

Freddy, besides being a very clever detective, was also a very accomplished poet, and it was plain from the delicate way in which he sniffed at a buttercup as he looked at them that he was in one of his poetic moods. For as everyone knows, a buttercup has no smell, and so it was evident that he was sniffing it for effect, and not because he got any pleasure out of it.

"I wish you'd cough when you come up behind us like that," said Alice a little sharply. "You quite startled us."

Freddy smiled dreamily and looked up into the sky as if he were listening to music. Then he began to beat time slowly with one fore trotter, and said:

"Hour after hour, day after day,
  I know just what everyone's going to say.

"Day after day, week after week,
  I know what they'll say before even they speak.

"Week after week, month after month—"

He broke off at this point and said: "You see, ladies, I know just how you feel."

"Oh, do finish the lovely poem, Freddy," said Emma.

"You liked it?" said Freddy, flushing with pleasure. "That is very gratifying. But I'm afraid I could hardly finish it now—that is, not properly. Perfection, you know—we poets must aim for perfection. Of course I *could* finish it, but—"

"Is there a rhyme for 'month,' Freddy?" asked Emma innocently.

"Dozens of them, my dear, simply dozens," he assured her. "But one must choose the best —the exactly right one. Poetry is not an easy thing. H'm, no indeed. Hard, brain-racking work. Sometimes, after finishing a verse, I am so exhausted that—" He stopped. "But I mustn't bother you with my professional troubles. What is it that seems to be the matter, Alice?"

"Oh, I don't quite know, Freddy," said the duck. "I'm tired of doing the same things over and over. I'd like a change. I'd like to take a trip. I'd like—" She hesitated, then brought it out, primly, but with determination. "I'd like to have adventures!"

"Sister!" exclaimed Emma with horror. "Oh, sister; how can you say such dreadful things?" And she began to cry.

"Well, I don't know," said Freddy; "that is quite understandable. I've often felt the same way. And I really don't see why you shouldn't do it, if you want to."

"But you're a pig, Freddy," sobbed Emma. "You're so brave and resourceful. We're only ducks!"

"Only ducks?" exclaimed Freddy. "*Only* ducks! Why, that reminds me, there's something I wanted to tell you about, that I read the other night in my encyclopedia. You know on the Fourth of July, in Centerboro, they're going to have a balloon ascension. They have one every year. They fill a big balloon with gas, and it has a basket hanging under it, and then a man gets in the basket and the band plays and the balloon goes up in the air. And by and by it comes down again in the next county or somewhere. Well, I thought I'd read up about balloons, and what do you suppose I found out? Who do you suppose was the very first living creature to go up in any balloon, anywhere?"

"Mr. Bean?" asked Alice.

"No, no; this was long before Mr. Bean's time over in France. There was a man named Mont— Mont— Well, I won't give you his name because he was a Frenchman, and of course his name is in French and you wouldn't understand it. Well, anyway—"

"Do say it in French," interrupted Emma, who had stopped crying. "Such a pretty language, I always think. And I'm sure you have a fine accent."

"The name is unimportant anyway," said Freddy firmly. "Now this, er—Frenchman made a big balloon, and when it sailed away up into the sky, who do you suppose was in the basket?"

Alice and Emma shook their heads.

"A duck!" said Freddy.

"Dear me!" said the sisters together. "Really? A duck!"

"Exactly," said the pig. "A brave and fearless duck. The first living creature to fly. The first aviator. And you say you're *only* ducks! You ought to be proud of your duckiness."

"What was her name?" asked Alice, and Emma said: "Did she come down safely?"

"History does not record her name," said Freddy, "but she did come down safely, and was, I have no doubt, rewarded for her gallantry with the highest honors. I should tell you that she was not alone in the basket; a rooster and a sheep were also passengers, but according to the encyclopedia they did not behave very well. At least when he came down the rooster had a broken leg because the sheep had kicked him. So we can assume that the duck was the only one that remained calm and unafraid. From what I know of you both I can only guess that she must have been an ancestor of yours."

Alice and Emma tried to look worthy of so heroic an ancestor, and Alice said: "I'm sure our Uncle Wesley wouldn't have hesitated to go up in a balloon."

"Dear Uncle Wesley!" said Emma. "He was *so* courageous!"

"Pooh," said Freddy, "I knew your Uncle Wesley, and I don't remember that . . . Well, let's put it this way: I think you're just as courageous as he was. I tell you what, Alice. That balloon man is a friend of the sheriff's, and the sheriff is a great friend of mine. How would it be if I spoke to him and got him to take you up with him the Fourth?"

"Take *me* up?" said Alice. "Well, gracious, Freddy; I don't know that I—"

"You wanted to have an adventure," said Freddy. "And here's one all ready-made for you."

"Why that's — that's — I mean — " Alice quacked excitedly. Then she closed her bill with a snap and drew herself up. "Very well," she said determinedly; "I'll do it."

"Sister!" exclaimed Emma in horror. "Oh, you couldn't!"

"And why not, pray?" said Alice. "I guess if a French duck can do it, an American duck can."

"But the balloon might be carried for miles; it might be carried out into the ocean by the wind. It might blow up."

"Well, if there's one thing I can do, it's swim," said Alice. "I've never had much practice flying—we domestic ducks aren't like the wild ducks—but if I fell out, I have my own parachute." And she spread her wings and fluttered them.

"Really, sister, you quite terrify me," said Emma in a faint voice.

"No reason for that," said Freddy. "I'm sure she'd be quite safe. And it would indeed be an

"Sister! . . . you couldn't!"

adventure. Yes, I may say that it has an attraction even for me. I've always wanted to fly."

"Oh, would you go up too?" asked Alice. "That would be very nice. We could make up a party, and take a picnic lunch—"

"Well, really," said Freddy, "if it was any day but the Fourth, I'd be delighted. But I have some—er, rather important engagements on the Fourth. And then, too, I weigh a good deal more than you do. The balloonist man might be willing to take a duck up with him, but I'm afraid a pig—no, I'm sure he'd object. Better not propose it to him at all. He'd very likely refuse you too, then."

"Oh, dear," said Emma; "sister, if you do want to have adventures, as you say, why can't you have them on the ground. You know how terrified I am of heights."

"But you don't have to go up."

"Naturally, I should insist on going," said Emma decidedly. "Why, we always do everything together, Alice."

"Then see if the man will take two ducks up, Freddy," said Alice.

"Oh, dear," said Emma, "I know I shan't enjoy a minute of it."

Freddy laughed. "No," he said, "you won't. That's the funny thing about adventures. I've had my share of them in my time, as you know, and my experience is that either you're too busy to think whether you're enjoying them or not, or else you're just scared. And yet there must be something about them that you like, too, or else you wouldn't go on trying to have more. But the nice thing is afterwards, with the crowds and the cheering and your picture in the paper and all."

"I shouldn't care to have my picture in the paper," said Alice. "Uncle Wesley always thought it was rather vulgar."

"They never look like you, anyway," said Freddy consolingly.

So after a while he left them, and that afternoon he walked down to Centerboro. At the jail he found the sheriff and some of the prisoners having a candy-pull, and he had to wait until the candy was cut up into lengths and rolled up in pieces of oiled paper before the sheriff could

go over to the fair grounds with him. Mr.
Golcher, the balloonist, was busy spreading out
his balloon on the ground and getting ready for
the ascension. He was a thin, rather sour looking man, but he shook hands with Freddy politely when the sheriff introduced them.

"So you're one of the talking animals from
the Bean farm," he said. "Glad to meet you."
Then he shook his head. " 'Tain't right for
animals to talk, though," he said. "Against
nature."

"Freddy's my good friend, Golcher," said the
sheriff. "Don't go picking on him."

"Say no more," said Mr. Golcher; "say no
more. Any friend of the sheriff's a friend of
mine, whether he be man, beast or insect;
whether he talks, sings or merely grunts. What
can I do for you, Mr.—er—"

"Just call me Freddy," said the pig, and explained his errand.

"Two ducks, eh?" said Mr. Golcher. "Well
now, Mr.—er, Freddy, I'll tell you. The balloon business ain't what it was. It's hard to get
a crowd for an ascension nowadays, what with
everyone wantin' to see nothing but airyoplane

flights. Balloons is going out, that's the truth of it. Now you're offerin' me a pair of ducks to take up with me, and I'd like to oblige you, but it ain't enough. Two ducks goin' up in a balloon—that ain't anything to draw a crowd. —But hold on!" He struck his forehead sharply with the palm of his hand. "Golcher has an idea." He looked sharply at the pig. "I expect you've made speeches in your time. Something of an orator, if what I hear is so, eh?"

"One of the finest public speakers in the county," said the sheriff warmly.

"Oh, well; I wouldn't say that!" said Freddy blushing.

"Fine," said Mr. Golcher. "That's how we can get our crowd. Ha, that'll bring 'em out. Patriotic pig makes Fourth of July address at balloon ascension. Think you could do it, Mr. —er Freddy? A good, roarin' patriotic speech just before the balloon goes up. Bringin' in America, and the flag—and balloons, of course. Think you could do that?"

Freddy had a sudden picture of himself, standing on a platform before a cheering crowd, with a flag waving overhead and a band ready to play when he had finished. "You bet!" he said enthusiastically.

"Good. That's champion, that is. Pig orator makes balloon ascension. I'll get me out some handbills right away, and those two ducks, they can go along with you as sort of trimming—they won't add nothing. But as long as they want to go—"

"You mean I'm to—to go *up?*" interrupted Freddy.

"That's just what Golcher means. Golcher has said so, and Golcher never goes back on his word."

"Well," said Freddy, "I don't know. The Fourth is a pretty busy day for me, and I don't know that I could spare the time. It's very nice of you, Mr. Golcher, but—"

"Eh?" said Mr. Golcher. "I don't get it. You said you had time to make a speech. You ain't afraid, are you?"

Freddy was indeed very much afraid. To see Alice and Emma go up in a balloon was one thing—after all, they had wings; but to go up himself was something different. He'd got himself into a nice fix.

But before he could say anything more, the sheriff said with a laugh: "Afraid? My friend Freddy afraid? I guess, Golcher, you don't know much about this pig's record." And he went on to make a list of Freddy's brave deeds for the benefit of the balloonist.

And as Freddy listened he began to perk up. It's true, he said to himself; I really have done all these courageous things. I guess I can't just back down now. That's the trouble with a reputation for bravery: you have to live up to it. Oh dear, I wish I wasn't such a fearless character!

So when the sheriff had finished, and Mr. Golcher had expressed his gratification at being privileged to know such a celebrity, Freddy said why of course he would go up in the balloon. And then after making some necessary arrangements, he and the sheriff left.

Chapter 2

When the animals on the Bean farm learned that Freddy and the two ducks were going to take a balloon trip on the Fourth, they were very much excited. A number of them came and asked Freddy if they couldn't go too. Freddy thought most of them were rather relieved when he said it couldn't be arranged. But they all planned to go over and see the ascension, and Mrs. Wogus, one of the cows, was appointed chairman of the refreshment committee, to see that a nice lunch was put up and taken along. Of course the Centerboro Fair Grounds was too long a walk for some of the smaller animals, so Hank, the old white horse, said he'd get hitched up to the phaeton that they had taken with them on the trip to Florida, and the mice and the chickens and any other small animals could get a ride.

Freddy spent nearly all day on the Third looking through his encyclopedia, and trying to find out how far the balloon might be expected to travel before it came down again. He didn't look in the encyclopedia very often, and like everything else in his study, which was in the front part of the pigpen, it was pretty dusty. When he turned the leaves the dust went up his nose and made him sneeze, and then he would lose his place and have to turn back and try to find it, and that would make him sneeze again, and then when he found the place his eyes would be watering so he couldn't read what it said. So he didn't get much information. But he kept at it, and by four in the afternoon he did know a little more than when he started.

He knew that nobody could tell where a balloon would come down.

So he put the encyclopedia away and blew his nose and went over to see Charles, the rooster.

Charles was sitting on a fence post in front of the henhouse. "Hello, Freddy," he said rather distantly.

"Hello, Charles," said the pig. "I suppose you've heard about this balloon ascension tomorrow?"

"Who hasn't?" said the rooster. "Anybody'd think nobody'd ever gone up in a balloon before, to hear 'em talk."

"Oh, sure," said Freddy. "It doesn't amount to anything. Only thing I'm worried about is this speech I've got to make. I'm no good as a speaker. Now if they only had you to make one of your good rousing patriotic orations—that would be something."

"Oh, you'll make a good speech all right," said Charles. "Of course, you haven't had the practice I've had, and maybe you aren't as eloquent as I am, but you'll do all right."

Now what Charles said was perfectly true. When Freddy made a speech he said what he had to say and sat down. But when Charles made one, he said everything he had to say in six different ways, each more high-sounding, and with bigger words, than the last one. On days when Charles was to give an oration, animals came from miles around to shout and applaud and wonder how he could go on and on in such beautiful language without saying anything of importance at all. For a funny thing about Charles' speeches was that though they were so stirring at the time, when you got home and thought them over you couldn't remember what they were about.

"Well, I don't know," said Freddy. "I'd hate to disappoint Mr. Golcher, and yet I'm afraid I'll make a poor job of it. I'd like the balloon ride all right; it'll be wonderful. But the important thing is to have the occasion a success, and with me as the principal speaker . . . Well, I tell you, Charles; much as I hate to pass up this wonderful experience, I've decided that you are the one who really ought to make the speech and go up. I've made up my mind for once to be unselfish about something, and to step aside and let you have the honor."

"H'm, very generous," said Charles, without much conviction. "But it doesn't seem to me that it would be fair. You were the one that thought up this thing, and arranged it— Of course," he said, "I could make the speech, and then you and the ducks—"

"That wouldn't do," said Freddy. "Whoever speaks has to go up. And another thing: you're a more suitable person, because it was a rooster, along with a duck and a sheep, that was the first living creature ever to fly. So the honor should be a rooster's, not a pig's. No pig ever flew."

But Charles said no. "I wouldn't feel right about it, Freddy," he said. He looked very noble and self-sacrificing for a minute, then he winked at Freddy, and edging closer along the rail fence he said in a low voice: "No, Freddy, my boy; I guess you're stuck with it."

"I guess I am," said Freddy to himself as he walked back home. "Oh, *why* am I such a fearless character?"

Two other volunteers for the ascension presented themselves, however. Unfortunately, as they had voices that could only be heard for about two inches, neither of them could take

Freddy's place. They were Mr. and Mrs. Webb, the spiders.

Quik, one of the mice who lived in the farmhouse, came down to the pigpen just before supper time to tell Freddy that the Webbs wanted to see him. Since it was an hour's hard walk for Mr. Webb from the house to the pigpen, he usually asked one of the mice to go for Freddy when he wanted to talk to him. The pig found the Webbs in a crack between two boards on the back porch where they usually waited when they had an engagement with one of the farm animals. He put his snout down and they climbed up on it, and then, trying not to tickle, walked up close to his ear.

"How about taking us up on this balloon trip, Freddy?" said Mr. Webb. "Couldn't you smuggle us aboard?"

"I don't see why not," said the pig. "But—are you sure you'd like it? We may be carried hundreds of miles before we get to earth again."

"We went to Florida, didn't we?" said the spider. "And we'd like to get away. We both need a change—mother particularly. She's been trying to shake that cough ever since early spring. And you know how it is: you can't catch flies if you begin to cough every time you try to creep up on one."

So Freddy said all right, he'd pick them up if they would ride over to the fair grounds in the phaeton with the other animals.

Usually on summer mornings Freddy woke up as quickly as possible and dashed off to the duck pond to take his morning dip with the others. But on the morning of the Fourth he tried to wake up as slowly as possible. First he just listened. That rushing sound—could it be rain? He tried to pretend it was rain and to go back to sleep, but he knew that sound too well—it was wind in the treetops. Wind! And he was going up in a balloon!

But maybe it was cloudy! He opened one eye and looked at the window. But the eye didn't tell him anything, because the window was so dirty that from the inside it always looked as if a storm was coming up. He opened his other eye, sighed, and slowly crawled out of bed. And then he saw a streak of sunlight under the door.

Now of course Freddy could have run away,

or he could have pretended that he was sick or something like that, but he was not that kind of a pig. If something unpleasant had to be done, he did it. He just wanted to be sure first that it really *had* to be done. So now he went over to the looking glass and tried different expressions on his face, to see which one would be the most suitable for the occasion.

Of course pigs don't wear regular clothes, so all Freddy had to put on was an expression when he got up in the morning. And on important mornings it often took him longer to dress that it would you or me. For he had a good many different expressions. When he went down to the First Animal Bank, of which he was president, he wore the "serious-pig-with-grave-responsibilities-on-his-shoulders" expression. When he was doing detective work, he wore the "keen-eyed-pig-who-misses-nothing" expression. And when he was writing poetry the one he put on was the "dreamy-poetic-pig." This morning he hesitated between the "intrepid-pig-who-scoffs-at-peril" and the "pig-who-is-about-to-go-up-in-a-ballon-and-thinks-nothing-of-it." They were a good deal alike, so he combined the two and wore them both.

The resulting expression was one of such iron determination that it greatly impressed all the animals with whom he talked that morning. "Why you aren't scared at all, Freddy," said Mrs. Wiggins, the cow. "Land sakes, you wouldn't get me to go up in one of those contraptions."

"Pooh, you wouldn't be any more scared than I am," said Freddy truthfully.

He hung around the barnyard most of the morning, enjoying the admiration and congratulations of his friends, for he felt—very sensibly, I think—that he might as well get all the glory he could out of the ascension beforehand, in case he drifted out to sea and was never heard of again. And when, after dinner, the animals set out for the fair grounds, he and the two ducks rode in the place of honor, in the back seat of the phaeton.

The Bean animals were very popular in Centerboro, and Freddy bowed and waved to many old friends as they went along through the fair grounds to where the balloon, now almost fully inflated with gas, was tugging in the breeze at the ropes that held it to the ground. The sideshows and the merry-go-round were almost deserted, for everyone had crowded up to listen to Freddy's speech and see the ascension. Mr. Golcher greeted them warmly.

"How's this for a crowd?" he said. "We're going to have an ascension today that *is* an ascension! And these are the two ducks? Happy to meet you, I'm sure. And all these are your friends? Golcher welcomes you, one and all."

On the ride over from the farm the two spiders had climbed up on to the top of Freddy's head, where they had prudently anchored themselves to a few strands of web spun between his ears. But when Mr. Golcher had led Freddy and the ducks over and helped them into the basket which was swung from cords that formed a net over the bulging surface of the balloon above them, the spiders found a safer place in a crevice of the basket, where they would be out of the way and still see all that was going on.

"Now," said Mr. Golcher, "you want to know what all these things are for. This here cord is attached to a valve that lets the gas out of the balloon. If you want to come down, you let a little gas out. If you're coming down too fast, you throw out some of these bags of sand, fastened along the side of the basket. If you're drifting along close to the ground and want to stop, you throw out this grapnel," he said, picking up a thing that looked like a sort of four-pronged anchor, which was fastened to the end of a coil of rope.

"But we don't need to know about those things," said Freddy. "I mean, you'll know better than we would what to do."

"I would if I was with you," said Mr. Golcher.

"You don't mean you're going to send us up *alone*?" said the pig.

"Why, sure. 'Twouldn't draw a crowd if I just took a pig up with me. Pig goes up alone—there, now you've got something." He took a handbill out of his pocket. "That's the way we advertised it, see? 'See the Flying Pig! Daring animal aeronaut braves dangers of the stratosphere! Hear the talking pig! Accomplished porker delivers patriotic address. Witness this breath-taking, super-stupendous phenomenon —the first and only quadrupedal orator and

"This here cord is attached to a valve . . ."

balloonist will make a balloon ascension at four P.M. sharp.' and so on and so on.''

"That's very nice," said Freddy. "Only I've never—er, driven a balloon."

"I'm sure you'll drive it very capably, Freddy," said Alice calmly. She and her sister were sitting on the edge of the basket, watching the crowd.

"Oh, dear," said Emma; "are you sure it's quite, quite safe, Mr. Golcher?"

"Be still, sister," said Alice severely. "Of course it isn't safe. But it won't be any safer if you tremble all over. What would Uncle Wesley say if he could hear your bill chattering?"

"I'll try to stop it," said Emma. "Oh, here's that nice sheriff."

The sheriff, who had come over to the fair grounds with some of the prisoners, came up and wished Freddy a pleasant journey, and handed him a large paper bag. "Some of the candy the boys pulled yesterday," he said. "They thought you might like something to chew on when you're chargin' around the sky."

At a signal from Mr. Golcher the band began to play. "Soon's the band stops," he shouted to

Freddy, "we'll begin to cast off the ropes, and while we're doing it, you make your speech. Then we'll let her go."

Freddy nodded mournfully, then almost absent-mindedly he opened the bag of candy and unwrapped several pieces and put them in his mouth. They were good. He started to chew them—that is, he closed his jaws down on them. But when he tried to open his jaws again, he couldn't. His upper and lower teeth were stuck as tight together as if they had been glued. And just then the band stopped playing.

The crowd gave a cheer and looked expectantly at Freddy, while the men began casting off the ropes that held the balloon to the ground.

"Your speech!" whispered Mr. Golcher. "Make it! You've only got three minutes."

"Mmmmmmm!" said Freddy, rolling his eyes, and the muscles on the sides of his jaws stood out as he tried to pull them apart.

"Speech! Speech!" shouted the crowd, and Alice said: "Freddy, what on earth—?"

"Mmmmmmmmmmm!" said Freddy, pointing to his mouth.

"I dunno what's the matter," said Mr.

Golcher angrily, "but by gormly, it's the last time I ever make a business deal with an animal!" He turned to the sheriff. "Look at him! *Your* friend, that's so brave—and he's so scared he can't talk!"

Freddy shook his head violently. "Mmmmmmmmmmm!" he said.

Some of the rougher elements in the crowd, who did not know Freddy very well, began to shout: "Boo! Boo!" while others, who had heard a good deal about his past exploits, shook their heads mournfully.

"Well, if you won't make a speech, I will!" exclaimed Alice. She flapped her wings. "Ladies and gentlemen—" But the crowd was making so much noise now, some attacking and some defending the pig's failure to speak, that no one heard her.

"Let her go, then!" shouted Mr. Golcher.

And with a rush the balloon shot up into the air.

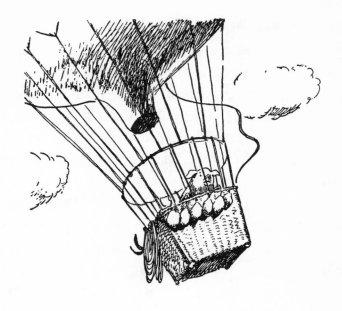

Chapter 3

Freddy, leaning over the edge of the basket, saw the crowd drop away beneath him. There was no feeling of going up into the air; it was as if the earth was falling away from the balloon. One minute the fair grounds were spread out beneath them, and then they shrank rapidly, slid away sidewise, and below was only a sort of colored map, in which fields were no more than green and brown squares, and the barns and houses, red or white dots, with roads like pieces of string connecting them. It was rather exciting, but not frightening at all.

Up where they were in the sky, the wind was stronger than it had been on the ground, and it carried them along swiftly. Emma had got down inside the basket, but Alice still sat on the edge, hanging on to a rope with her bill. "Look, look! Here comes the Bean farm!" she exclaimed, and sure enough, over the horizon came rolling the familiar fields and woods, with the tiny white house and barns and stable and hen-house . . . "And that little speck you can hardly see is my home," thought Freddy. "Oh, when will I enter it again?"

"Why, there's the duck pond, that little blue dot," said Alice. "Sister, come up here; you're missing everything."

"I'm all right here," said Emma miserably.

"Oh, come up! What would Uncle Wesley say to such talk!"

"I'll hold on to you so you won't fall," said Freddy, who had at last got the better of the candy and found his voice.

"Oh, dear—all right," said Emma faintly. And then when they had got her up on the edge beside Alice: "Why, it—it's quite pleasant!" she exclaimed delightedly. "Dear me, not at all alarming! I suppose that moving speck out in the hayfield is Mr. Bean. What time do you think we'll get home, Freddy?"

"You may get home sooner than you expect to unless you stop talking and hang on to this rope," said Alice.

"I think perhaps we ought to go down a little," said Freddy. "We're pretty high up, and we don't want to be carried too far." And he gave a short tug at the valve cord.

But nothing happened.

"That's funny," he said. "Mr. Golcher said you didn't have to let much gas out if you wanted to come down."

He gave two longer pulls, and then as the balloon still kept on at the same level, he called: "Hey, Webb! Come up here a minute."

The spider came up over the edge of the basket and climbed up by Freddy's ear. "We've been riding on the bottom of this thing," he said. "My word, what a view!"

Freddy explained what was the matter. "I wish you'd climb up this cord," he said, "and see if that valve works."

So Mr. Webb climbed up, and in a few minutes he climbed down again and reported that the valve cord had got tangled in some of the ropes so that the valve couldn't be opened. "Guess there's nothing you can do," he said. "I'm not strong enough to fix it, and you're too heavy to climb up."

"My goodness, do you see what that means?" said Freddy. "We can't get down."

"She'll come down some time," said the spider unconcernedly. "Anyway, you can always jump. No, no; I'm just fooling, Freddy. But what's the use of worrying?"

"But suppose she comes down in the middle of the Atlantic Ocean?"

"We're being blown away from the Atlantic Ocean at about thirty miles an hour," said Mr. Webb. "I'm hoping we'll be over Niagara Falls in the morning. Mother and I have always wanted to visit the Falls." He walked down to the end of Freddy's snout and dropped from it to the edge of the basket.

"What's that you've got on your back?" asked the pig, for on the spider's shoulders—or at least the shoulders of his first pair of legs—was a little bunch of something grey that seemed to be fastened around him with strands of web.

"Parachute," said the spider. "Mother spun a couple of them for us to take along. Kind of foolish, I thought. But you know how women are."

"H'm," said Freddy. "You and Mrs. Webb have parachutes, and Alice and Emma have wings, but what have I got?"

"My goodness, you've got one of the finest views below you a pig ever set eyes on. Why don't you enjoy it and stop worrying?" And the spider disappeared over the edge.

The view was indeed impressive. Directly below them now was a good-sized lake, set among rolling hills, wooded towards the tops, but laid out on the lower slopes and in the valleys in different colored shapes of cultivated land like a jigsaw puzzle. At the end of the lake was a tiny white village, and off in the distance, to the northwest, a big city sprawled under a smoky haze. Syracuse, Freddy thought.

He discovered suddenly that he was enjoying himself. He had only been scared because he had thought he ought to be scared, but after all he was having one of the most remarkable experiences of his long and colorful career. Of course, there was that speech he hadn't made; people were going to criticize him for that. But he could deliver a speech when he got back that would make them forget that unfortunate incident, or he wasn't Freddy.

The balloon drove on westward. They were over Syracuse now; they could see strings of cars moving through the streets like ants; and an airplane came up and circled them twice and then flew away. Alice and Emma waved their wings excitedly at the pilot, who waved back. Syracuse rolled off down over the eastern horizon. "Next stop, Rochester," called Alice.

"And the next one is Buffalo," said Freddy, and then he became thoughtful. For he had an idea that the next stop after that would be Lake Erie, and while it wasn't as big as the Atlantic Ocean, it wasn't a place he wanted to stop at on a balloon trip. He wished he had brought his geography along.

By and by the sun began to go down. The shadows of the hills grew longer and longer,

The view was indeed impressive.

and they flowed together and darkened the roads and the fields and the villages, and finally covered them with a dark blanket, although the balloon, high up in the air, was still in the bright sunlight. Little lights pricked out here and there on the earth, some of them moving along the roads, others stationary in windows. And then the sun slid down out of sight.

It got cool. Alice and Emma jumped down inside the basket.

"I'm hungry," said Emma.

"My goodness, I hope there's something to eat here," said Freddy. He rummaged about. "Cans!" he said disgustedly. "Soup, beans, corned beef. Can opener, too. But what good is that?" For though he was very clever with his trotters, and could run a typewriter and even write with a pencil, he couldn't hold a can opener with them. "Well, we've got that bag of candy, anyway."

So they ate the candy for supper. They didn't talk much while they were eating it, but when they could open their jaws again Freddy said: "It's going to be cold up here, and there's nothing more to see tonight, but we've got a blanket, and I vote we get under it and go to sleep."

So they did. And Freddy was just dozing off when he felt a tickle in his ear and Mr. Webb's voice said: "Getting kind of chilly for mother out there, so we thought we'd crawl in with you if it's all right."

"Sure, sure," said the pig. "Only thing is, aren't you afraid you'll get squshed? If I was to roll over in the night—"

"Well, we'd rather not be squshed, and that's a fact," said Mr. Webb drily. "But you've got good roomy ears, Freddy. Suppose we sleep in one of them? We'll be very quiet."

"Yeah?" said Freddy. "And suppose you get to thrashing around in your sleep? Suppose you fell down into my ear and couldn't get out? It makes me shudder to think of it. No, I'm sorry but that's just out. Hold on, though. Ducks don't lie down when they sleep; they just stick their heads under their wings. Suppose you get in with them—under the other wing? Nice and snug, and no danger. Real feather bed."

So the Webbs fixed it up with Alice to get in under her left wing, and then they all went to sleep.

When they awoke next morning the balloon was drifting along over rough and heavily wooded country. There were no villages in sight, and only here and there in a clearing a ramshackle house. They were much nearer the ground now, because in the cool night air the gas in the balloon had condensed so that it wasn't as light as it would be later when the sun heated it up again. At least that was how it was explained to Freddy later, though at the time he just thought they had begun to come down. The basket wasn't more than a hundred feet from the ground, though it might as well have been a thousand, Freddy thought, as far as getting out was concerned.

"It's funny," said Alice; "I wonder if we went over Buffalo in the night? And if we did, I suppose we're in Ohio."

"It's too rough for Ohio," said Freddy. "And look—there's a mountain. There aren't any mountains in Ohio. The geography says so."

"Maybe the geography is wrong," said

Emma. "Dear me, there is the mountain to prove it."

"It's very odd," said Alice; "we were going towards the sun when it set last night, and now it's rising and we're still going towards it."

They puzzled over this for some time, until Emma said excitedly: "Why we're going east! And that's because the wind has changed in the night. It's carrying us in the other direction."

"Oh," said Freddy. "Oh, of course. Should have thought of that myself. I expect I would have in a minute, when I got waked up."

"What you'd better think about when you get waked up," said Alice, "is where we're going to get breakfast."

"My goodness!" said Freddy, and fell back against the side of the basket. For if there was anything he *didn't* like it was going without his breakfast. Or for that matter any other meal that it happened to be time for. Or even indeed anything to eat whether it was time for it or not. The world of the sky in which they were adventuring was a wonderful world, but if it was a world without food it was no place for him. "We've got to get down," he said.

"If we have to get down to get breakfast," said Alice, "I prefer to go without breakfast. I'm not hungry enough to jump."

"There's one piece of candy left," said Emma.

So they decided to divide up the piece of candy, and when they had eaten that they could think about what to do next. But it isn't easy to divide up a piece of molasses candy if you haven't got a knife, or scissors or anything. The ducks took the paper off, and then they each took hold of an end and pulled. They pulled and pulled, but all that happened was that the piece of candy got longer. They pulled it until it stretched from one side of the basket to the other, and then of course they couldn't go any farther. They couldn't stop, either, because they had taken such a firm hold that they couldn't get their bills open again. So Freddy took hold in the middle, and then the ducks ate towards him, and pretty soon they were all sitting there with their noses together, trying to chew. And in that way they ate up the piece of candy.

When they could talk again, Alice said:

"Dear me, I wonder why it is that as soon as your jaws get stuck tight together you think of so many important things to say?"

"I did too," said Freddy. "And now I can't remember any of them."

"Uncle Wesley always used to say," quacked Emma, "that most of the things people thought of to say were better left unsaid. He said if you took all the talk that went on on this farm during a year and squeezed it out, you wouldn't get more than two drops of sense."

"As I remember your uncle," said Freddy, "he was quite a talker himself."

"A very fine talker," said Emma. "He said many wise things."

"Wise, eh?" said the pig. "You ought to collect them in a book. You could call it 'Wise-Quacks.' 'Uncle Wesley's Wise-Quacks.' Hey, that's not bad!"

But the ducks didn't laugh, and Emma said primly: "I don't think Uncle Wesley would like that."

Freddy tried to explain. "A duck quacks," he said, "so a duck's wise-crack is a wise-quack. I mean, it's a—"

"Uncle Wesley did not approve of slang," interrupted Alice. "He said it was the empty rattling of a brain too small for its skull. Were not those his words, sister?"

"His very words," said Emma.

"And quite right, too," said Freddy quickly. "Well, let's just—er, drop the whole thing." He was getting a little tired of Uncle Wesley, whom he remembered as a stout and pompous little duck who had ruled his nieces with a rod of iron. Long after they had grown up, "what Uncle Wesley said" was their law, and they would no more have thought of doing anything of which he disapproved—and he disapproved of practically everything—than they would have thought of becoming burglars.

Freddy remembered something more about Uncle Wesley, too. For a band of the farm animals, who were fond of Alice and Emma and sick of seeing them tyrannized over, had kidnaped him one night and turned him over to an eagle, who for a small consideration had agreed to drop him somewhere in the next county. Freddy had not had a hand in that plot. But with his great detective ability he had of course found out about it, and while he didn't approve of such highhanded action, he didn't make any effort to get Uncle Wesley back. For after all, Alice and Emma would be much happier without him.

But they admired him so intensely that even after his mysterious disappearance had freed them from his tyranny they continued to quack his praises and to do as they thought he would approve. His fearlessness, his polished manners, his high moral standards, his deep wisdom— they praised these things daily. Freddy didn't believe that anybody, even a pig, could reach such a height of perfection.

Chapter 4

As the sun got higher the breeze died down and
the balloon hardly seemed to move. It rose
higher as the sun got hotter, but it wasn't as
high as it had been yesterday, and they could
see quite clearly everything that went on below
them. Once, when the shadow of the big gas
bag drifted across an untidy barnyard, a flock
of chickens ran cackling for cover, and a woman
came to the house door and stared, shading her
eyes with her hand. A little stream ran out of
the woods and across the foot of the garden and
into the woods again. And in it were what

looked like several large powder puffs.

"Ducks!" exclaimed Alice. She leaned over the edge of the basket. "Mercy me, sister, if that doesn't look for all the world like Uncle Wesley!"

"Why, it does indeed," said Emma. "He has just that same aristocratic way of holding his head. You don't really suppose . . ?" The ducks stared at each other.

Freddy, who had been hanging on to their tail feathers so they wouldn't fall, tried to look too, but the balloon had drifted on. "It's not likely to be him," he said. "From this height all ducks look alike."

"Not Uncle Wesley," said Emma proudly.

"We have always thought, Freddy," said Alice, "that if we had come to you when Uncle Wesley first disappeared, you could have restored him to us. But of course then you hadn't taken up detecting."

"I could probably have found him," said the pig modestly. "But today, even if he hasn't been —that is, I mean, if he is still, er—"

"There is no need to try to spare our feelings," said Alice. "We are not afraid to face the dreadful possibilities of what might have happened. If he has not, you mean, been eaten by a fox, or—"

"Oh, sister!" quacked Emma faintly.

"—or a cat," continued Alice firmly. "But if some such thing had not happened, he would have returned to us, or at least sent some word."

"Perhaps he got married," said Freddy.

"Oh, I'm sure he would at least have sent us an announcement," said Emma.

"We feel," said Alice, "that he must have set out on some dangerous adventure. Perhaps he did not tell us, because he did not want us to worry. And he was so utterly without fear; he would not have hesitated to fight anything that walks or flies, if he felt he was in the right. Do you remember, Emma, the time he ordered that bull out of the cornfield?"

The ducks went on with their reminiscences of their intrepid uncle, and Freddy stopped listening and leaned over the edge of the basket and watched the scenery and thought about scrambled eggs and hot buttered toast and muffins with jam and other things that the people in the houses below them were probably having for breakfast at that very moment. I don't know that you can blame him. One third of a piece of molasses candy is not a very filling breakfast.

Suddenly a large bird came soaring over the top of a distant hill, then swerved and with powerful wing beats came flying towards them. He was dark, with a white head and tail. "Good gracious," said Freddy to himself, "an eagle! I do hope it isn't Pinckney. That would be just too much of a coincidence when we've been talking about Uncle Wesley." For Pinckney was the eagle who had carried the ducks' uncle off.

Like all birds, the eagle was curious, and he wanted to investigate the balloon. Pretty soon the ducks caught sight of him, and with frightened quacks they cowered in the bottom of the basket. The eagle was so close now that they could hear the swish of air made by each down stroke of the great wings. And then he caught sight of Freddy, and with a harsh scream of surprise turned a complete double somersault in his amazement at seeing that the balloonist was a pig.

He recovered himself fifty feet down, and beat up to their level again. "Welcome, oh pig, to the starry upper spaces of the blue empyrean," he said as he soared alongside. "What strange chance brings you thus to adventure in your frail chariot among the trackless haunts of the feathered folk?"

Freddy had talked to eagles before, so he was not surprised at this high-flown language. Eagles, since they are the national bird, have a great sense of their own dignity, and feel that just ordinary talk is beneath them.

Freddy, however, was pretty good at noble-sounding language himself. "Hail, oh monarch of the skies," he said, and then explained about the ascension and their present difficulties. "And so," he concluded, "we know not where we are, nor whither we are bound, nor are we provided with the wherewithal to sustain life on this problematical and involuntary journey. Therefore we beseech your aid. If your present course should lead you within wingbeat of the domicile of that respected farmer, Mr. Bean—"

"Mr. Bean!" interrupted the eagle, and he swung in towards them, and perching on the

Freddy blushed.

edge of the basket, stared at Freddy with his fierce yellow eyes. "Great is the renown and widespread the repute of that excellent man, Bean, and his talented livestock among all furred and feathered dwellers within the confines of the Empire State. And you—ha! those well-weighed words I should have recognized. Are not you that pig whose noble song in praise of the eagle is taught to every young eaglet throughout the length and breadth of these mountains before he is allowed to leave the nest?"

Freddy blushed. "I did indeed, five years ago, pen some few poor lines in unworthy tribute to our national bird. But I had thought them long forgotten."

"Forgotten!" exclaimed the eagle. "Ha, you should hear my young Waldemar recite those glowing stanzas. How does it go?

"O eagle, mightiest of all living things,
Nor Death, nor Destiny, has longer stings—"

"—spreads stronger wings," corrected Freddy. "Of course. And then:

*"Thy claws of steel, thy beak of burnished brass
Make malefactor pigs chew up the grass."*

"That's not just exactly as I wrote it," said Freddy. "Though very nice. But I wrote:

*"Thy claws of brass, thy beak of burnished steel
Make malefactor pigs in terror squeal."*

"Ah, yes," said the eagle. "But in either version, most complimentary. And while written, as I am given to understand, specifically for my brother Pinckney, a most elegant compliment to the entire eagle race."

"Pinckney is your brother?" inquired Freddy. "I trust you will present him my compliments, and ask him, when he has leisure, if he will do me the honor of paying me a short call. There are matters on which I wish to consult him."

"Ah, I do remember," said the eagle, "that there were certain business transactions between Pinckney and various of your associates. Concerning a goose, was it?—or a—"

"*If* you please," interrupted Freddy quickly, and with a gesture indicated the two ducks, who were pretending to be powder puffs, with their heads under their wings.

The eagle cocked his head and stared at them with his left eye. "Eh?" he said in a harsh whisper. "Ah, I see. The nieces? Ha, yes; you can trust me." He lowered his voice. "There is a farm in South Pharisee owned by a Mr. Pratt. I fancy that inquiries there may be fruitful.—And now, my friend," he said aloud, "in what can I serve you? Your high poetic talent, and your remarkably true and exact portrayal of eagle character, command my service. Instruct me, I pray."

So Freddy told him what he wanted. It took a lot of language, which would occupy too many pages here, so I will not repeat it. But when the eagle finally took his leave, he had promised to tell the animals at the farm of their plight, and to arrange somehow for them to get something to eat. After that Freddy felt better.

Chapter 5

The eagle, whose name was Breckenridge, had told Freddy that they were now over the northern Adirondacks and headed for Lake Champlain. But the wind was almost gone. Slowly and more slowly they drifted, and at last hung nearly motionless over a long narrow lake, the wooded shores of which were almost solid rows of summer cottages and camps. Pretty soon people caught sight of the balloon, and came running down off their porches with opera glasses and telescopes, and shouted and waved. But this was getting to be an old story to the balloonists now, and they hardly troubled to wave back.

Early in the afternoon Freddy saw a speck in the southern sky which he at first took to be an airplane, but which, as it grew steadily larger, he saw was the eagle.

"Look, Alice—Emma," he said excitedly. "Here comes Pinckney's brother. Oh, I do hope . . . Yes, he's got a hamper." And sure enough, in his strong talons the eagle was carrying a large hamper whose contents were covered with a white napkin.

"How's he going to give it to us?" asked Alice. "If he perches on the edge of this thing, he'll have to let go of the hamper first. And if he keeps hold of the hamper, he can't stop."

Apparently Breckenridge had just had the same thought. He soared in circles around the balloon two or three times, then shouting hoarsely to Freddy to catch hold, he came in closer, beating his wings in swift strokes to hover motionless beside them. Freddy leaned out as far as he dared, but he couldn't reach the hamper, for Breckenridge's wings were so big that he couldn't come in any closer without hitting the ropes.

He dropped away from them on a long slant, then came past again. "Devise something, pig; devise something," he called.

"My goodness," said Freddy, "what can I devise? Oh, dear, there's our dinner right in plain sight, and it might just as well be in California.—Oh, wait!" he exclaimed suddenly. "The grapnel!" He picked up the four-pronged anchor and lowered it over the side until it hung some ten feet below them, then took a turn of the rope around a cleat and waited. The eagle, with a harsh scream of approval, swooped down and hung the hamper on one of the hooks, then flew up to perch beside Freddy and help him haul it up.

The hamper tipped dangerously as they pulled it over the side. "Careful, pig," said Breckenridge. "Let not your native greed overmaster caution. No need to share these viands, prepared for you by the capable spouse of the worthy Bean, with the finny folk in the waters below us.

"You are indeed an accomplished porker," he went on, as they swung the hamper to the floor. "I feared for a time that my errand was in vain."

"You're pretty accomplished yourself," said Freddy modestly; "and pretty kind, too, to take all this trouble for us." He was so hungry that he could hardly talk, but he felt it wouldn't be very polite to start eating until he had thanked Breckenridge.

But the eagle snatched the napkin off the hamper with his beak. "Your courtesy," he said, "should be a lesson to all quadrupeds. But now let courtesy give place to appetite."

There was a note under the napkin. It said:

Dear Freddy:

I am sending just what I could get together quickly. I would have baked a cake, but if you are hungry you would not want to wait. Come home as soon as you can. We miss you. Mr. Bean sends kindest regards.

Your friend,
Mrs. Bean.

"Well, that is nice," said Freddy. "And now what have we got? H'm, cookies, doughnuts, peach preserves, a pail of milk, deviled eggs—" But I am sorry to say that when he had got this far in his catalogue of the hamper's contents, his mouth was so full that the rest of what he said was not understandable.

The ducks had overcome their fear of the eagle, and they each began nibbling a cookie.

"Won't you join us, Mr. Breckenridge?" said Emma timidly.

"I would consider it an honor," replied the eagle, and immediately gobbled up six deviled eggs, one after the other, whole. "Very tasty," he remarked, and ate four doughnuts. "A most accomplished culinary artist, the excellent Mrs. Bean," he added, and spearing a jelly sandwich with his beak, tossed it in the air, caught it and swallowed it in one motion.

"How clever!" exclaimed Emma. She tried to do the same trick, but the sandwich flew out of her bill and over the side.

"Careful," said Freddy. "We may be up here a long time, and we'll need all this food."

But the eagle, flattered by Emma's admiration, continued to do the trick until eight jelly sandwiches, four bananas, and six slabs of gingerbread had disappeared.

Freddy began to be worried. At this rate they'd be out of supplies again before supper time. Yet he didn't like to say anything, when Breckenridge had been so helpful. Fortunately the eagle himself began to realize that he was eating more than his share, and suddenly putting down a cinnamon bun that he was about to toss up, he said with some embarrassment: "My good friends, I make you my apologies. I am presuming upon your hospitality."

"Not at all, not at all," said Freddy. "It is a very slight return for your great kindness."

"You are the very pattern of politeness," replied Breckenridge, and for several minutes they continued to exchange compliments. It was probably one of the most polished exchanges which has ever taken place in a balloon. Indeed Freddy was so exceedingly courteous that he almost persuaded the eagle to eat up the rest of the provisions. At this point, luckily, Alice interposed. Perhaps, she suggested, they

She tried to do the same trick . . .

could make Breckenridge some return for his service which would be not quite as ordinary as just something to eat.

Freddy couldn't think of any reward for any service which could be better than something to eat, but he saw the point. "I have it," he said. "I will write another verse for him to my Ode to the Eagle."

Breckenridge was delighted with the idea, and Freddy, who was always at his best as a poet after a good meal, began thinking. And in a few minutes had his verse.

"The fearless eagle cleaves the stormy air;
  With mighty wings he sweeps the clouds
    asunder;
He screams defiance at the lightning's glare,
  And at the thunder's crash he laughs like
    thunder."

Breckenridge had Freddy repeat the verse several times before he would make any comment. Then he said: "My friend, aside from being one of the finest compliments ever paid our race, I do not believe that Shakespeare himself could have achieved a loftier flight of fancy.

'Flight of fancy'—ha! Not bad, eh? 'The fearless eagle tum te-tum te-tum—'' What rhythm! What sweep! And that phrase: 'at the thunder's crash—' ''

A distant low grumble interrupted his words. He turned sharply and peered up at the sky. Black clouds were piling up over the wooded hills, and a gust of wind sung through the ropes and set the basket swaying.

"Thunder!" muttered Breckenridge. "I—ah, h'm, dear me; I'm afraid I must be going. My little Waldemar—alone in his nest, you know. Mother away. Visiting her aunt this weekend. Well, see you later." And he spread his wings and dropped from the edge of the basket. In a minute or two he had vanished in the northern sky.

"That's funny," said Freddy. "Fearless eagle, eh? And scared of thunderstorms. He was scared, you know."

"And so am I, Freddy," said Emma, as she watched fearfully the boiling cloud masses that crept over the sun.

"Well, I am too," said Freddy. "But there's nowhere to go. We'll just have to ride it out.

We'd better snug down as well as we can. I'll call the Webbs."

The spiders came up over the edge of the basket, and Freddy found them a cozy refuge from the storm in one of the oiled paper envelopes the sandwiches had been wrapped in. He put the envelope in the hamper, then he and the ducks covered themselves up with blankets and ponchos, and having tucked themselves in carefully, waited for the storm to break. Which it presently did with a blinding flash and a crash as if the whole sky had fallen in on them. The basket gave a lurch as the wind struck it; the rain pelted like hundreds of drums on the stretched rubber of the balloon; and then swaying and jerking crazily, balloon and basket, pig and ducks and spiders, went careering off through the lightning slashed darkness.

Chapter 6

It was a wild ride the animals had through that
thunderstorm, and it lasted a long time. For of
course they went along with it. When you're
on the ground, a storm will come up in one part
of the sky and drive pouring and roaring above
you, and then go grumbling off over the hills
in another part of the sky. But when you are in
a balloon, you drive along with it. It seemed to
Freddy as if there were a dozen thunderstorms,

and that the balloon would be carried like a football by one of them for a while, and then passed to another, and then another. It lurched and swung dizzily, with ominous creaks and crackings that could be heard plainly above the hiss and rattle of wind and rain. Freddy expected any minute to have the whole thing torn to pieces around them.

But at last the storm blew itself out. The thunder stopped rolling, the rain slackened, and the motion of the basket grew quieter. Fortunately the ponchos had kept them dry. Freddy crawled out to look around. But although the sky was clearing, the sun had set and it was too dark to see much. He got some sandwiches from the hamper and he and Alice ate their supper. Emma had a sick headache from the motion, and didn't want any. Then he opened the oiled paper envelope to see if the Webbs were all right.

"My, my, what a trip!" said Mr. Webb. "Mother's quite done up; I think perhaps now things have quieted down we'll stay right here and try to get some sleep."

"I think we all need sleep," said Freddy. And

as the ducks agreed with him, they curled up again under the blankets in the bottom of the basket.

Perhaps because of the buffeting it had taken from the storm, which might have knocked some of the gas out of it, the balloon was now much nearer the ground than it had been before, and the grapnel, which Freddy had forgotten to stow away after he had pulled up the hamper, barely missed by inches the tops of the taller trees over which they drifted. Indeed, once or twice during the night it caught for a second and then pulled free again, and at those times the sharp jerk of the basket woke Freddy up. But he was too sleepy to get up and investigate, and after waiting a minute to see if anything else happened, he dropped off again.

But a little before daylight a sharp jerk woke him again, and this time it was followed by a series of tugs that tipped the basket and sent him and the two ducks and the hamper and Mr. Golcher's box of canned goods into a heap in one corner. At first when he got out he couldn't see much, partly because the sun was not yet up, and partly because in the struggle of getting out of the blankets Alice had stepped in his eye. But it was getting lighter all the time, and pretty soon he made out that the grapnel had caught under the eaves of a house and was holding them anchored there, only a few feet above the roof.

There was something familiar about that house, and about the barn and the yard and the gate.

"Have either of you girls ever seen this place before?" he asked, as the ducks hopped up beside him. He always called them girls when he thought of it, because it both pleased and flustered them a little. It pleased them because it made them seem younger than they really were, and it flustered them because it didn't seem quite dignified. Of course, they weren't very old, but for ducks they were really grown up.

"Why no, Freddy," said Alice. "We haven't, have we, sister?"

"We've never been in the Adirondacks before," said Emma.

"I think we've been blown out of the Adirondacks," said Freddy, "though where we are now

I don't know. It just seemed to me I'd seen it all before."

"Why, now you mention it," Alice began, and then she stopped, for an upstairs window opened in the house, and a head came out and twisted around to look up at them, and then a mouth opened in the head, and yelled: "Hey, pa!"

"Down!" whispered Freddy. "Keep out of sight. Oh, I know where we are now, all right."

"So do I," said Alice, "and I don't like it, Freddy."

Indeed, there was a very good reason for them not to like it. On their famous trip to Florida, they had had some trouble, as you may remember, with a man with a black moustache and a dirty-faced boy. On the way back home, Charles and Henrietta had been captured by these two, and would have been eaten for Sunday dinner if the other animals hadn't succeeded in rescuing them. And now, the face that was looking up at them . . .

"Are you sure that's the same boy, sister?" Emma asked.

"I'm sure it's the same dirt," said Alice. "There's the same black smudge on his left cheek. Why, he can't have washed his face in five years!"

"Disgraceful!" said Emma.

The boy, followed by the man with the black moustache, who was his father, had come out into the yard and was staring up at the balloon.

"That must be the balloon you heard about last night over the radio, pa," said the boy. "The one that pig went up in that the police are hunting for."

Freddy pricked up his ears.

"You get a rope, sonny," said the man, "and climb up on the roof and hook it to that anchor thing, and then we'll pull it down."

"If that pig is the robber, and we get the reward the police are offering for him," said the boy, "will you take me to see the circus over at South Pharisee, pa?"

"Maybe yes and maybe no," said the man. "You wait till we get it down and see what's in it."

"There ain't anything in it."

"Oh, yes there is," said the man. "The pig's

in it. I can see the tips of his ears."

"Is that the pig that talks, pa?"

The man laughed coarsely. "He won't talk much when we put an apple in his mouth and pop him in the oven." He turned suddenly and cuffed the boy. *"Go get that rope!"*

"Didn't I hear Breckenridge say something to you about South Pharisee?" Emma asked Freddy.

"My goodness, I don't know. What difference does it make? Did you hear what the man said?"

"You needn't be so cross," said Emma. "They'll eat us too."

Freddy shuddered. "Don't *talk* like that! Don't you realize that to escape from here I've got to have all my wits about me, and how can I when you keep talking about we're going to be eaten up? It—it unnerves me."

"Hush, sister," said Alice calmly. "Let Freddy think."

So Emma hushed and Freddy thought. And he really did think of something. He took hold of the grapnel rope and unfastened it from the cleat. At first he was going to let the grapnel and the rope both go, but the other end of the rope was tied to the basket in a knot that it would take some time to untie, and besides, he didn't want to lose the grapnel if he could help it. So he waited until the breeze slackened a little, and then he loosened the rope and gave it a quick shake. And the grapnel came free and the balloon started slowly away from the house.

At this the man with the black moustache, who had been watching with a superior grin on his face, gave a loud yell and ran into the house. The balloon, which was moving very slowly, was only halfway across the next field when he came out again with a gun and began to run after it.

"He's going to shoot us," said Alice. "Oh, Freddy, I wish we could get out and push."

"All he's got to do is hit the balloon," said Freddy, "and the gas will come out and down we'll come."

The man had caught up and was nearly under them now, but as he pulled up the gun to shoot, Freddy snatched two cans of beans out of the box of canned goods and threw them quickly down at him, one after the other. The

. . . the second can hit a rock and burst.

first one hit the gun, which went off with a bang, and the charge of shot whizzed harmlessly by the balloon. And as the man opened his mouth to yell, the second can hit a rock and burst, showering him with baked beans and tomato sauce, some of which went right into his mouth.

"Help! I'm being bombed!" he shouted, and threw himself flat on his face in the hay. Then he licked his moustache. "Beans!" he exclaimed thoughtfully, and was starting to get to his feet again when he saw the tomato sauce all over his shirt, and then he gave a very loud yell and fell down even flatter than before.

Freddy hadn't realized it, but the weight of two cans of beans makes quite a difference in a balloon, and when he threw them out, the balloon went up quite a lot higher in the air. They still weren't out of gunshot, but the man with the black moustache was so sure that he was mortally wounded that he lay still until the dirty-faced boy came out and helped him to his feet. And when he found out that he wasn't wounded after all, he cuffed the dirty-faced boy good. He did this for three reasons: first, because the balloon had got away; and second, because he would now probably have to take a bath to get the tomato sauce off him; and third, because it seemed like a pretty good thing to do anyway. And I don't say they were good reasons, but that is what they were.

In the meantime the balloon had sailed off across two meadows and a hill, and Alice and Emma were praising Freddy. "You saved our lives," they said.

"Pshaw!" said Freddy modestly. "That's nothing."

"Our lives may be nothing to you," said Alice tartly, "but they are pretty important to us."

So Freddy apologized. He wasn't quite sure what he was apologizing for, but as a general thing, if anybody expects an apology, the polite thing is to give it to them. It saves a lot of wear and tear.

Although their adventure had been pretty terrifying, one thing they had learned through it: they were not very far from home.

"The storm must have blown us back towards Centerboro," said Freddy. "If we could get down now, we could be home by suppertime. What do you say: shall we let down the grapnel and try to hook on to a fence or a tree? Then maybe we could pull the balloon down and get on the ground.''

The two ducks looked at each other. Then Emma said: "If you want to go home now, Freddy, Alice and I are willing. But—" She hesitated. "Why, dear me," she said, "if anyone had ever told me that I should really enjoy being blown around the sky, and half starved, and thundered at, and chased by men with guns, I wouldn't have believed them. Our Uncle Wesley enjoyed that kind of thing, but Alice and I have always been home bodies. Of course I have been simply terrified a good deal of the time, but now that I am not terrified any more —well, sister, what do you think?"

"I think you are showing a spirit of which Uncle Wesley would be very proud," said Alice. "For myself, I came out to have adventures, and if there are any more to be had, I say—have them. I am quite willing to continue our voyage for a time."

"Well, that's fine," said Freddy. "We don't need to ask the Webbs: they're game for anything, I know. Now there is one reason why I would prefer not to go home right away, and that is that apparently the police are looking for us. That means that Mr. Golcher thinks we have stolen his balloon, and has got out a warrant for our arrest. If we go home now, the police will catch us and put us in jail, and nobody will believe our explanation that the valve cord wouldn't work. But if we bring the balloon back to Mr. Golcher ourselves, or at least leave it somewhere and then find him and explain, I think everything will be all right. Because there's a lot of difference between being arrested with the stolen goods in your possession, and returning them to the owner yourself."

"The police are undoubtedly looking for us," said Emma. "Look down there."

They were passing over a road, and as Freddy looked he saw a white police car beside which stood two state troopers. They were looking up and waving their arms and shouting, and although the balloonists couldn't hear what they were saying, there was no misunderstanding what they wanted. One of them even pulled out a pistol and fired two warning shots.

"We'd better just pretend not to understand," said Freddy, and he leaned over and waved and nodded. The troopers shook their fists and motioned, but Freddy pretended to misunderstand, and he continued to wave and even blow kisses until the balloon had drifted over the next hill.

"I'm afraid you have made them very angry," said Emma.

"Well," said Freddy, "they can't prove I knew what they wanted. My goodness, lots of people wave to us."

"They don't shoot pistols," said Alice.

"They probably would if they had them," said Freddy. "And now let me see; that road down there runs west into Centerboro, and then northwest to the farm. The wind is taking us a little to the north of that, into the hills above Centerboro. So let me tell you what I plan to do, and see if it meets with your approval."

Chapter 7

It was late in the morning before the balloon drifted over a place that Freddy thought would do for the plan he had in mind. It was a cleft between two heavily wooded hills. He let down the grapnel as far as it would go, and it disappeared into the treetops, and then there was a tug and he knew it was caught fast. He took a turn of the rope around the cleat, and every time there came a lull in the breeze and the balloon stopped pulling, he would haul in a little of the rope, and thus pull them down towards the earth. Ducks aren't very strong and they aren't built for pulling anyway, but they helped as much as they could.

"It's like—pulling in a big—fish," panted Emma. "Only we're—pulling in the earth. I don't suppose—anybody ever caught—a bigger fish than that."

"Maybe we could catch the moon next," said Freddy. "We could hang it up in the barnyard, and then Mr. Bean wouldn't have to pay any more electric bills."

"We'd better make sure of the earth first," said Alice, "before we plan anything else."

It was hard work and slow work, but at last the balloon was pulled down until the basket was anchored just above a thick limb that grew halfway up a big oak. Then Freddy threw out the rope ladder and climbed down it. The end of the ladder was a good six feet from the ground, but Freddy only hesitated long enough to say "Oh, dear!" and then dropped.

I know that they say it doesn't hurt fat people to fall as much as it does thin people, but it hurt Freddy all right. He bounced three times, and the first bounce made him yell, and the second bounce brought the tears to his eyes and the third bounce made him grunt. And then he lay still for a minute watching what looked like Roman candles going off in all directions. He looked around to see if his legs were all in place, and then he got slowly to his feet.

"Oh, Freddy, are you all right?" Emma called.

He looked up and saw the ducks peering anxiously over the edge of the basket.

"Sure, I'm all right," he said bravely. "So long, and don't expect me back before tomorrow night." And he limped off into the woods.

After he had gone a little way he felt better. He kept his shadow on his right and trudged steadily southward, for that was the direction in which the Bean farm lay. After a couple of hours he came out of the woods into the open fields. In front of him was a broad valley, dotted with farmhouses and laced with roads, and on the other side of the valley, perhaps four miles away, the woods began again. These, he knew, were the Big Woods, where he had once hunted the strange and terrible Ignormus, and beyond the Big Woods were Mr. Bean's woods, and then the farm. But how was he to get across this open valley without running the risk of being seen and captured by the police?

Back at home, in what Freddy called his library, which was really just a shed built on to the back of the pigpen, were dozens of disguises, all neatly hung on hangers, which he used in his detective work. In any one of these he felt sure he could walk straight down the road without the slightest danger of being recognized. But without a disguise he was just a stray pig, and if the police were really looking for him, any stray pig was bound to be stopped and questioned.

It was while he was hesitating at the edge of the woods that he saw the scarecrow. It stood in a field of young corn not far off. It was better dressed than most scarecrows, for it had on a long-tailed black coat and striped trousers, and on the head, which was a piece of white cloth tied around a bunch of hay, was a high silk hat. The whole thing was stuffed with hay, and held up by a stake, with a crossbar along which the arms were fastened. It was pretty well made, but

". . . I'll bring everything back tomorrow."

whether it would really have scared crows much is another matter. Crows are not easy to fool.

Freddy looked all around but nobody was in sight, so he ran down quickly into the cornfield, and in two minutes the scarecrow was just two sticks and Freddy was a very dressy little man who looked as if he might just have come from a wedding. "I'm sorry to do this," he said to the sticks, "when somebody has taken so much trouble to fix you up, but I'll bring everything back tomorrow." He shook the straw out of the head, and tied the cloth around his neck like a stock, and then he drew on the white cotton gloves, gave the top of his hat a tap to settle it over his ears, picked up the crosspiece for a walking stick, and started down to the road. There was only one thing missing; the shoes. If he met and talked to anybody, he must remember to stand in the grass.

For a while everything went very nicely. The people he met stared a good deal, and in the one village he passed through, several little boys followed him, making remarks, for as a usual thing, people as fashionably dressed as he was ride in large shiny automobiles, and do not walk along country roads. But he strode along, twirling his stick, and tipping his hat politely to the ladies, and nobody bothered him.

Now Freddy had never worn a high silk hat before, and he was naturally anxious to know how he looked in it. But there weren't any plate glass windows in the village, and he couldn't go up to a house and rap on the door and say: "Please may I admire myself in one of your mirrors?" Yet people were so respectful to him that he thought he must look pretty nice. So a little way past the village he came to a pond, and he went over to it and crouched down at the edge and tried to see himself in the water.

Well, he bent over too quickly, and the hat fell into the pond. So he fished it out and dried it on the grass, and after the ripples had cleared from the water he tried again. He bent over very slowly, but each time, just before he could tip his head far enough over to see his reflection, the hat began to slip.

Then he tried holding it on. But the sleeves of the coat were much too long and too wide for him, so that although he could see the reflection of his face, the sleeves fell forward and hid the hat. And at last he gave it up.

A little farther on he came to a barn, and on the side of the barn was a big poster advertising a circus. It showed lions and tigers and bareback riders and clowns, and in big red letters across the top it said: BOOMSCHMIDT'S COLOSSAL AND UNPARALLELED CIRCUS, and in smaller blue letters at the bottom it said: South Pharisee, Week of July 6th.

"So *that's* the circus the dirty-faced boy was talking about!" said Freddy to himself. "Oh dear, why couldn't Mr. Boomschmidt have come through here later in the season? If I didn't have all this balloon business on my hands I could have gone to South Pharisee, wherever it is, and seen the show and had a good time with all my old friends. But I guess it's out of the question now." He thought for a minute. "South Pharisee. Wasn't that the town Breckenridge mentioned, where he thought we might find Uncle Wesley? H'm, that should be looked into."

Mr. Boomschmidt, the owner of the circus, was an old friend of Freddy's, as were many of the animals in his show. Indeed, Freddy had once done him a great service, and as Mr. Boom-schmidt was not the man to forget a service, however small, the Bean animals were always sure, not only of free tickets to all performances, but of all the lemonade and popcorn they could hold, whenever the circus came anywhere near Centerboro, as it did about once a year. Freddy was mournfully looking at the poster and picking out the pictures of his friends: Freginald, the bear, and Leo, the lion, and all the others, when a car drew up on the road behind him and a voice said: "Morning, stranger."

Freddy knew that voice. It belonged to his friend the sheriff. But Freddy did not turn round. For he knew that if there was a warrant out for his arrest, as the dirty-faced boy had said, the sheriff would have to do his duty and arrest him, no matter how good friends they were. So he only turned halfway around and saluted with his walking stick, and said in a deep voice: "Good morning, sir; good morning."

But the sheriff didn't drive on. He got out and came and stood beside Freddy. He didn't look at the pig, but just stood staring at the poster and pulling at his wisp of grey beard.

And after a minute he said: "Stranger in these parts, aren't you?"

"I am, sir, and my name is Jonas P. Whortleberry," replied Freddy, making up the first name that came into his head.

"Dear me," said the sheriff; "not one of the Albany Whortleberrys?"

"Distantly related, I believe," said the pig. "My own home is in Orinoco Flats," he added, making up another name.

"Fine, thriving community, I'm told," said the sheriff.

"My goodness," thought Freddy, "I wonder if there really is such a place?" But it was such fun making up names, that he could not resist the temptation to go on. "I am just returning from my daughter's wedding in Ishkosh Center," he said. "My car broke down some distance back, and since, as the head of an important banking house, I get far too little exercise, I am walking on until my chauffeur effects the necessary repairs, when he will, I presume, overtake me."

"May I ask your chauffeur's name?" inquired the sheriff.

"Herman Duntz," said Freddy without hesitation.

"Ah, yes. Good sound stock, the Duntzes. My wife's third husband was a Duntz."

This remark puzzled Freddy a good deal. In the first place, the sheriff wasn't married, and in the second place, if he had been, could he have been his wife's fourth husband? And in the third place, there weren't any Duntzes anyway.

"I think I must be getting on," he said. "Good day to you, sir."

But the sheriff continued to stare at the poster without looking at Freddy, and then he said thoughtfully: "Yes, yes. So must I. You haven't," he said suddenly, "seen a pig anywhere up the road, have you? A handsome, decidedly intelligent looking pig?"

Freddy, remembering the difficulty he had had trying to see just such a pig in the pond, said truthfully that he had not.

"Ah," said the sheriff. "Perhaps it is just as well. You see, I'm the sheriff, and while this pig is a good friend of mine, I'm looking for him, and if I see him—" He hesitated a minute.

"—if I *see* him," he repeated, "I'll have to arrest him. Stole a balloon, they say."

"That—that's a funny thing to steal," said Freddy uneasily.

"I can't figure it out," said the sheriff. "This pig—he's as honest and open as the day. Well, sir, you're a man of the world; I'd like your opinion. This pig—" And he told Freddy the story of the balloon ascension. "He was to bring the balloon down in a mile or two," he concluded, "but he didn't; he just disappeared— pig, balloon, ducks,—the whole kit an' bilin' of 'em vanished off the face of the earth. And this Golcher, he's pretty mad. Naturally. The balloon's his means of livelihood, and he was to get $200 for an ascension at Boomschmidt's circus day after tomorrow. But what I can't figure is what a pig, even a criminal pig, which this Freddy ain't—what he'd want with a balloon."

"Very odd business," said Freddy, in his deep banker's voice. "But I understand that these balloons are very tricky affairs. Isn't it within the bounds of possibility that something went wrong? That, let us say, the valve cord got stuck, so that this—Freddy, I think you said?—couldn't get down?"

"Hadn't thought of that," said the sheriff. "Yes, it might be. Well, sir, it's a bad business. Now if *I* was that pig—" He broke off. "But I'm keepin' you, botherin' you with my affairs—"

"Not at all," said Freddy. "Pray continue."

"Well, if *I* was that pig, I'd stay with that balloon, somehow, until I could bring it back and deliver it to Golcher myself. That'll prove your—that is, the pig's good intentions. Once he's picked up by me, or the state police, it's jail for him, and he can explain until he's blue in the face—nobody'll believe him. Even if he don't get sent to prison, even if he gets off, people are always going to say: 'That's the pig that stole the balloon; keep your hand on your pocketbook.' So my advice to him is—that is, my advice would be, if I could advise him, which of course I can't, being out to arrest him—well, anyway, he hadn't ought to try to go home. The police are watching the farm day and night." He stopped abruptly and pulled out a silver watch as big as a saucer. "Must be gettin' on," he said, and turned away.

Then he stopped and came back. "By the way," he said, "if you got time, you ought to see this circus. Lions and tigers and fat ladies and performin' snakes and land knows what all. First right and four miles straight ahead to South Pharisee." He looked thoughtfully at the poster. "I expect that's where I'd head for if I was that pig. He's a great hand at disguises, and if he was to get himself up in something—oh, like what you got on, for instance; plug hat and tail coat and so on, I expect he'd be as safe there as anywhere. Golcher may be there, but Golcher is pretty nearsighted. If the pig didn't go right up and kiss him, I guess Golcher wouldn't ever recognize him. Well, good morning to you, sir."

Freddy looked after the sheriff's car as it bounced up the road. The sheriff hadn't looked at him once. "My, he's a nice man," said Freddy.

Chapter 8

When he came to the right hand road that led to South Pharisee and the circus, Freddy passed it without even turning his head. For if he turned his head, he knew he would turn the rest of himself, and then there he would be, marching right down towards the merry-go-round and the Ferris wheel and the clowns and the peanuts and all his friends— I mustn't think about it, he said to himself. Duty is duty, he said. And he twirled his stick and went on across the valley.

Early in the afternoon he came out of the woods into Mr. Bean's upper pasture. There was the duck pond, where usually Alice and Emma were to be seen sitting side by side, like two marshmallows on a mirror. There was the familiar house, with Mrs. Bean shaking a table-cloth out of the kitchen window, and there was Jinx, the cat, walking across the barnyard. It was Jinx he particularly wanted to see, and he started to wave one of his white gloves to attract the cat's attention when he stopped suddenly and crouched down. For off to the right, sitting under an apple tree in the meadow above the barnyard, were two state troopers.

Freddy began to wish that he had followed the sheriff's advice and gone to South Pharisee. Of course, if he had really stolen the balloon, as the sheriff had apparently thought, it would have been good advice to follow. But he wasn't trying to escape from justice. On the other hand, he wasn't going to let the police catch him if he could help it. And he had to see Jinx. He took off his hat and wiped his forehead with the white glove and tried to think of something.

Now Freddy had a good deal of imagination, and people like that are apt to think up so many ways of doing a thing that they can't decide among them, and then they don't do anything. But he was also a pig of action, and so he discarded all the ideas that meant sitting around and waiting, and decided on the one that meant doing something right away. He scraped up some of last year's hay and tucked it into his sleeves and his neck and under his hat, then when the troopers were looking the other way he walked out into the pasture. And when they turned towards him again, what they saw in the pasture was a scarecrow, standing with his arms stretched stiffly out, and with wisps of straw stuffing sticking out here and there.

As soon as they turned their heads away, Freddy moved a little way down towards the barnyard, and then stood still when they looked in his direction again; and he kept on doing this until he had almost reached the fence which separated the pasture from the next field. He had only to cross this field, and he would reach the fence that ran around the barnyard, and he was pretty sure he could sneak along behind the fence and get into the barn without being seen.

But all at once one of the troopers jumped up and, shading his eyes with his hand, stared hard in his direction. "That scarecrow has moved from where he was a minute ago, Bill," he said.

"Don't be silly, Wes," said Bill. "A scarecrow can't move."

"Well, this one has. First he was up by the woods, now he's almost down to that fence."

Bill got up. "Maybe somebody moved him," he said. "What's the difference! We're looking for a pig, not a scarecrow."

"Sure we are. But it's our duty to investigate anything peculiar, and I guess we'll never see anything peculiarer than a walking scarecrow. Because maybe it ain't a scarecrow after all."

"Peculiarer?" said Bill. "That ain't a word."

They began arguing about it, while Freddy stood motionless. His arms ached so it didn't seem as if he could hold them up another minute, and the hay in his coat collar and under his hat made him itch in seven different places, but he couldn't scratch them. He was just getting ready to bolt back to the woods if the troopers started towards him, when a woodpecker came flying across the pasture. Freddy said in a sharp whisper: "Hey! Sanford!"

The woodpecker looked around, banked sharply, and lit on the pig's shoulder. "For Pete's sake, Freddy, what are you doing out here in this get-up?"

"Trying to get to the barn without the police catching me. But I guess it won't work, and if I have to run for it, tell Jinx to meet me at the edge of the woods after dark, will you?"

"Sure," said Sanford. "But do you think they've spotted you?"

"I'm afraid so. But wait a minute—listen!"

Wes was saying: "But it can't be alive, I tell you. Do you suppose that bird would be sitting on it if it were alive?"

"Guess I saved you, Freddy," said Sanford. "Maybe we'd better make sure. Suppose I drill a couple holes in your hat, hey? That'll clinch it."

"It'll clinch me," said Freddy, with a nervous glance at the woodpecker's sharp beak. "No, no; this hat's pretty thin. I tell you what you can do, though," he added, as the troopers sat down again under their tree; "go tell the animals. Maybe they can think of some way of getting rid of those men."

Nothing happened for ten minutes, and they were the longest ten minutes in Freddy's life. His arms were getting numb now, and didn't hurt quite so much, but he had to watch them so they wouldn't just drop down all by themselves. In addition to the seven itches mentioned above, there were several new ones, and a fly had lighted on his nose. Freddy twitched his nose violently, but the fly just laughed and hung on. Then he walked slowly up the nose, dragging his feet.

Freddy knew that fly. His name was Zero, and at one time they had had a good deal of trouble with him around the farm, until they had got a wasp named George to discipline him. After that Zero had kept away from the barnyard, and Freddy hadn't seen him in some time.

At first Freddy asked Zero politely to get off his nose. The fly pretended not to hear him. Then Freddy ordered him off. Zero walked down to the end of the nose and looked all around. "Strange!" he said to himself. "I could have sworn I heard somebody speak!"

"Zero!" Freddy hissed. "Quit that tickling, will you? This isn't any time for your silly jokes."

"That certainly is queer," said Zero, and he began walking over Freddy's face, pretending to look for the voice. "I heard it, just as plain as plain. Must be somewhere." He looked in Freddy's eye, and in his ear, and he crawled up under the edge of the hat, and at last he walked down and peered up one of Freddy's nostrils. But this time he had overstepped, for at that precise moment Freddy's self-control gave way in one tremendous sneeze. It blew Zero twenty feet in the air and sprained three of his legs and one wing, and he dropped into the grass and lay there senseless for quite a long time.

Fortunately the men hadn't noticed the sneeze. They were looking rather doubtfully at three cows who were coming slowly towards them from the barnyard. The cows were Freddy's friends, and their names were Mrs. Wiggins and Mrs. Wurzburger and Mrs. Wogus. They came along slowly, pulling a bite of grass here and a sprig of clover there. They paid no attention to the troopers. They came up under the tree. And first Mrs. Wiggins stepped on Bill's hat, and then Mrs. Wurzburger swung her tail around and hit Wes in the eye, and then Mrs. Wogus nudged Bill aside with her big broad nose to get at a patch of grass. The troopers picked up their hats and jammed them on their heads, and hitched back towards the tree.

"Cows," said Wes. "Do they ever attack people?"

"What do you call this?" said Bill, crawling around behind the tree.

"I dunno," said Wes, crawling after him. "But I don't like it."

Mrs. Wiggins and Mrs. Wogus came around the left side of the tree, and Mrs. Wurzburger came around the right side, and they lowered their heads and stared at the men.

"They got nice kind eyes," said Wes.

"Yeah?" said Bill. "They got nice long horns, too. Hey!" he exclaimed. "Go on away, you— you animals, you. Shoo!"

But the cows came closer. Mrs. Wiggins gave a kind of deep muttering in her throat, and then

Mrs. Wurzburger and Mrs. Wogus shook their horns threateningly.

Bill got up. "I'm getting out of here," he said, and started down towards the farmhouse.

"Maybe you're right," said Wes, and followed him.

They walked slowly at first, and the three cows walked slowly after them, and then they went faster, and the cows went faster, and then they were running with the cows galloping after them. The cows roared ferociously as they galloped—at least it seemed ferocious to the troopers, although really the cows were just laughing. And when the troopers had jumped on their motorcycles and disappeared up the Centerboro road, they lay down in the grass and laughed until Mrs. Bean came to the back door.

"Shame on you," she said severely; "scaring those nice young men away! And stop that racket. Mr. Bean is taking his nap."

So the cows got up and went off to the cow barn, where they found Freddy.

Freddy sat on the floor, fanning himself with one of the white gloves. He looked pretty done up, but he brightened when the cows came in.

"How on earth," he said, "did you ever manage to scare those policemen away?"

"Land sakes!" said Mrs. Wiggins, "we knew they'd be afraid of us. You see, Freddy, if they'd been brought up in the country, they'd have known right away that no farmer would ever put up a scarecrow in a pasture. Scarecrows belong in cornfields. There's no sense in scaring crows out of a pasture, because there's nothing for them to steal. So we knew they didn't know anything about farm life, and we figured they'd probably be afraid of cows."

"Well, I call that pretty clever of you," said Freddy.

The cows looked down, and said "Thank you," bashfully. They weren't used to being praised, which I think is rather a pity, because cows are just as smart as other animals, only in a different way. But people seldom praise them to their faces—I don't know why.

"But, Freddy," said Mrs. Wiggins, "had you ought to be here? Mr. Bean is pretty mad at you for stealing that balloon."

"But I didn't steal it," said Freddy. "My goodness, all you animals are my friends, and

Freddy sat on the floor . . .

yet you always seem ready to believe the worst of me." So he told them what had happened. "And," he said, "I want to get Jinx to go over to see Mr. Golcher and explain to him. I can't do it, because he's mad at me, and as soon as he sees me he'll call the police. But if Jinx can tell him everything, and where the balloon is, then everything will be all right, and he'll call off the police."

"It would be better if you could get the balloon back to him yourself, wouldn't it?" said Mrs. Wogus. "I mean, if you really brought it back, then nobody could say you stole it."

"That's what I'd like to do. But—" He broke off. "What's all that noise?" he asked. For there was a lot of shouting and laughter going on over by the stable.

"Oh, it's those mice, I guess," said Mrs. Wurzburger. "Ever since they heard about the balloon ascension they've been crazy to fly, and they got Mrs. Bean to make them some little parachutes, and they've spent all their time jumping off the roof." She laughed. "Cousin Augustus was so excited about it that the first jump he made he forgot the parachute. But a mouse is so light that he can jump off a roof anyway without getting hurt much. I guess it just knocked the wind out of him."

"Sssssh!" whispered Mrs. Wogus. "Somebody coming."

Freddy went to the door and peered out. "Oh, gosh!" he said. For Mr. Golcher had just got out of a car at the gate and was coming towards the house.

Chapter 9

Mr. Bean, whose nap had been cut short by the laughter of the cows, came out the kitchen door just as Mr. Golcher started across the barnyard. Freddy saw the two meet and stand for a moment talking, and then Mr. Golcher handed Mr. Bean a cigar, and Mr. Bean smelt of it and put it in his pocket, and they went around and sat down on the front porch. Freddy hadn't heard anything they said, and ordinarily he was too polite to listen to conversation that wasn't intended for him, but he felt that this occasion was too important to let politeness interfere. So he went around the other side of the house, and crawled up through the shrubbery until he was close enough to listen.

"—and in my opinion," Mr. Golcher was saying, "unless the police catch him, he won't ever be heard of again."

Mr. Bean puffed on his pipe. "Dunno why anybody'd steal a balloon," he said.

"You ain't ever had one, have you?" asked Mr. Golcher.

Mr. Bean shook his head.

"Well, that's it. Take it from Golcher; Golcher knows. Balloons are queer. You get attached to 'em after a while. Like some folks get attached to horses or dogs. Now the way I figure it, this pig, he gets attached to this balloon, and he can't bring himself to give it up. 'Golcher?' he says. 'Who's Golcher? He can't ever catch me. Here I am up in the air, and I can go sailin' on the rest of my life.' He don't know the gas'll give out after a while, and he'll come down and won't be able to go up again because he don't know how to get more gas. Bein' a pig, he don't realize these things—"

"He ain't dumb," said Mr. Bean shortly.

"I know he ain't," said Mr. Golcher. "Not for a pig. But after all, he *is* only a pig—"

"I say, he ain't dumb," repeated Mr. Bean firmly.

"Well, suppose he does realize all those things," said Mr. Golcher. "I don't want to say more'n I can prove. But he did steal the balloon."

"He ain't a thief," said Mr. Bean.

Mr. Golcher didn't say anything for a minute. Mr. Bean puffed on his pipe and looked out placidly across the fields.

"Well," said Mr. Golcher finally, "so he ain't dumb and he ain't a thief. But where's my balloon?"

When Mr. Bean didn't know the answer to a question he kept still. He kept still now. Some people would have said they thought maybe it was this, or maybe it was that, but not Mr. Bean. For he knew what lots of people never learn: that no answer is better than the wrong one, and sometimes than the right one, too.

"Well," said Mr. Golcher, "you ain't much help, and that's a fact."

"Waitin' for your proposition," said Mr. Bean.

"My proposition?"

"You come here to see me. Must have a proposition to make. Well, make it."

Mr. Golcher looked at him sharply. "Well, now, he's your pig," he said, "and if I was to sue you for loss of business and the value of the balloon, you'd have to pay. Because any damage he causes is your responsibility."

Mr. Bean nodded. "Never denied it," he said.

"Oh, well, then," said Mr. Golcher, "there's no reason why we can't agree. There's the balloon gone, and there's five hundred dollars I was to get for the ascension at the circus tomorrow—"

"Two hundred," said Mr. Bean.

"Eh?" said Mr. Golcher. "Why two hundred wouldn't hardly cover the cost of—"

"Save your breath," interrupted Mr. Bean. "Two hundred was what Boomschmidt agreed on. Phoned him this morning to find out."

"Oh, well," said Mr. Golcher. "Let it go.

Golcher wants to be fair. Golcher ain't one to quibble over a dollar or two. Say two hundred for loss of business, and for the balloon—well, that's kind of hard to figure. That there balloon —well, sir, that balloon's more than just a balloon to Golcher. That's a balloon, you say—just a bag full of gas. But not to Golcher. That balloon and me, we been together now for fifteen years. We—"

"Pretty near wore out then," said Mr. Bean calmly.

"Wore out?" said Mr. Golcher. "No it ain't wore out; it's as good as the day it was first blown up."

"We ain't getting anywhere," said Mr. Bean. He dug down in his pocket. "Here's your two hundred. You lost that on account of my pig, and I'll pay it."

"But the balloon!"

"I don't buy any balloon," said Mr. Bean. "Suppose your balloon comes back tomorrow? Then I have a balloon on my hands, and what do I do with it?"

"Do with it? I guess, Mr. Bean," said Mr. Golcher solemnly, "if you'd had any experience with balloons, you wouldn't ask that question."

"Shouldn't have asked it anyway," said Mr. Bean, and he got up and held out the two hundred dollars.

Mr. Golcher counted it slowly. "But this only makes up for the ascension I couldn't make," he said. "It don't pay for the balloon."

"Pig'll bring it back, likely," said Mr. Bean. "If not, meet me in a week's time at Judge Whipple's, in Centerboro. We'll let the judge decide what I owe you." And he said good day and went into the house.

After Mr. Golcher had gone, Freddy went back to the cow barn. He was pretty pleased to find that Mr. Bean really believed in him, even though appearances were so much against him. He realized that, in spite of his gruffness and apparent indifference, the farmer was a real friend—much more of a friend than some of the animals who were always protesting their friendship. "I'll get that balloon back if it's the last thing I ever do," he said firmly.

But even if he got the balloon back, Mr. Bean was still out two hundred dollars, and how could he do anything about that? It was true, he had about seven dollars in the First Animal Bank, of which he was President, but it had taken him two years to get that together. "If it takes two years to get seven dollars," he said to Mrs. Wiggins, "how long would it take to get two hundred?"

"Seven hundred years," said Mrs. Wiggins.

Freddy didn't think that was right, and he tried to do it in his head. But the cows were trying to do it in their heads too, and they kept saying: "Seven goes into twenty . . . put down four and carry three . . . that's thirty-five plus eight," and things like that, until it is no wonder that he got a different answer every time. But as the lowest answer he got was thirty-seven years, he decided that there was no use going on with it.

But the cows went right on. Mrs. Wogus said she made it ninety-eight, and Mrs. Wurzburger thought it was only seventeen, but Mrs. Wiggins stuck to seven hundred. "It's only common sense," she said. "If you get seven dollars in two years, then in seven hundred you get two hundred."

"It sounds right when you say it," said

Freddy, "but I'm sure there's a mistake some-where. But anyway, if it only takes seventeen years, it's too long. So I'll have to think of some-thing else."

He sat down against the wall and tipped the silk hat over his eyes, and the cows looked at one another, and Mrs. Wiggins winked and said: "Come on, girls, if there's going to be some thinking done, it's no place for us." And they tiptoed quietly out.

And sure enough, in about five minutes Freddy really did think of something. It is true that in another minute he would have been sound asleep. But that is often the time, just on the edge of sleep, when people do think of the best things. The trouble is that they are seldom strong-minded enough to jump up and put their ideas into action at once. And so they drop off to sleep and the ideas are lost.

Freddy wasn't specially strong-minded, and perhaps he would have gone to sleep anyway, but just as he got the idea, his head nodded and his hat fell off, and that woke him. He jumped up and started to dash out of the door, just as Jinx, who had heard that Freddy was hiding in the cowbarn, started to dash in. And they met in the doorway and Freddy's hat was knocked off again.

As they started to pick themselves up, they both said crossly: "Hey, why don't you look where—" And then they stopped and said: "Oh, it's you."

"Sorry, old pig," said Jinx, and he picked up the hat and brushed it off and handed it to his friend. "Boy, that's a stylish outfit. Looks like you were invited to the White House to lunch. Where'd you steal it?"

"I didn't steal it," said Freddy coldly. "I borrowed it."

"Like you borrowed that balloon, I bet," said the cat. "Golly, you certainly got yourself into a real mess this time."

"I didn't steal the balloon either," said Freddy. "But there's no time to explain now. Listen, I've got to get out of here without being seen, and I want your help."

"Thought you wanted me to meet you tonight," said the cat. "Sanford said—"

"That's off now," said Freddy. "Got a better plan. Go get those mice over here. Tell 'em to

"Sorry, old pig," said Jinx . . .

bring their parachutes. And then you get Mr. Bean out of the way until I get started. He's in the stable, and he mustn't see me."

"O.K.," said Jinx. "But where you off to?"

"It's an adventure," said Freddy. "Tell you afterwards."

"Why don't I go with you then?"

"Oh, I don't know; it's kind of dangerous. I guess I can handle it better alone." Freddy very much wanted Jinx to go with him, but he knew that the surest way to get him was to pretend that he didn't. That's a cat all over. Let him think you don't want him to do something, and he's crazy to do it.

"Oh, come on, Freddy. You wouldn't leave me out, would you? Your old pal, that's stood at your side on a hundred battlefields? Jinx, the old tried and true, whom you know you can count on to the last whisker and toenail? Back to back, and bare teeth and claws, and bring on your lions and tigers! Eh, Freddy?—that's the old Bean spirit; that's the—"

"Oh, all right," said Freddy. "Anything so I don't have to listen to a pep talk."

"Yow!" Jinx yelled delightedly, and dashed out of the barn.

A few minutes later, the four mice—Eek and Quik and Eeny and Cousin Augustus—came running in. They dropped their parachutes, which they had been carrying in their mouths, and all began talking at once. "What's up, Freddy? What goes on? You going to give a show?"

"How'd you boys like to take a *real* parachute jump? From a balloon a mile high?"

"A real jump? Oh boy, what a chance! You bet! From a real, big balloon? Would we like it! Would we . . . Would . . ." They were suddenly silent.

"How far up, did you say?" asked Quik, in a voice which was small, even for a mouse.

"Well, maybe not a mile," said Freddy. "But good and high. My gracious, you don't mean to say you're *scared*?"

"No," said Eeny. "No-o-o. Not scared, exactly. Only—well, our aunt, you know—she lives over in Centerboro, and she—well, maybe she wouldn't approve."

"She's got funny ideas, you know Freddy," said Eek. "She doesn't like us to do things that are—sort of—showing off."

"Not-dignified things," said Cousin Augustus.

"Listen," said Freddy; "you haven't heard from your aunt in five years, and anyway, if I remember right she used to do slack-wire walking when she was younger, and if that isn't showing off . . . But of course, if you want to turn down a fine opportunity to win fame and fortune, it's nothing to me. Ducks go up in balloons, pigs go up in balloons, but mice—no, no; they're too scared. What Mr. Bean'll say . . . But there; forget it, boys. I'll get some rabbits."

The mice looked at one another. "Rabbits!" said Quik, then he jerked his head, and they all picked up their parachutes. "When do we start, Freddy?"

"That's the spirit," said the pig. "Get into my pockets, and I'll tell you more as we go along."

He looked cautiously out of the barn door. He had heard Jinx crying for some time, and now he saw that the cat was standing by his empty saucer on the back porch, and looking up hopefully at the kitchen door. Every now and then he would give a very piteous *meroooow*.

Pretty soon Mrs. Bean came and looked out. "I know what you're up to, you villain," she said. "But you've had your dinner, and there isn't any more for you."

"Give him something to eat, Mrs. B.," came Mr. Bean's voice from the stable.

"He's had his dinner," said Mrs. Bean, "and if I let him coax me into giving him more, he'll be teasing me all afternoon." And she smiled at Jinx and went back into the house.

"*Merooow*," said Jinx.

"*Meroooooow*."

"*Meroooooooooow!*"

"Oh, good *land!*" exclaimed Mr. Bean, coming out of the stable. "Stop that bellering. I'd rather feed you ten meals a day than have to listen to that."

"*Merow-row?*" said Jinx.

Mr. Bean bent down and scratched his ears, then picked up the saucer and went into the house. And as soon as he had disappeared,

Freddy jammed the silk hat down on his head and bolted out through the barnyard. He crossed the meadow, and was safe behind the fence below the pasture when Mr. Bean came out again. Then when Mr. Bean had put down the saucer of food before Jinx, and had gone back into the stable, he went on up towards the woods.

At the edge of the woods he waited for Jinx. He had to wait a long time, but at last the cat came.

"You might have hurried a little," he said.

"Chicken gravy," said the cat, licking his lips reflectively. "I will say this for Mr. Bean: he's no hand to pet his animals, but when he feeds 'em he feeds 'em."

They went on up through the woods. It was pretty hot, and Freddy had to sit down several times and cool off. The mice in his pockets kept wriggling around, and pulling themselves up and trying to see out; and every time they wriggled Freddy wriggled too, for they tickled. And at last he said: "You boys come out of there and get up on the brim of my hat. It's bad enough being tickled any time, but when you're hot and sticky, it's awful.'' So they did.

They came to the rim of the valley and started down across the fields towards the road. And they had almost reached it when up the road they heard a *Brrrrrr,* and saw two dots which got bigger and bigger and— "Get down in the grass, Jinx," said Freddy sharply, and he lifted his arms and held them out stiffly and stood motionless.

The two troopers came buzzing along on their motorcycles, but when they saw Freddy they stopped.

"Funny thing," said Bill, "but that looks like that scarecrow over at Beans'."

"Funny to see two with such grand clothes," said Wes. "Folks must have been pretty dressy around here in the old days."

Bill started to walk over for a closer look, but there was a deep ditch with water in it between him and the field, and he stopped.

"You know," said Wes, "to me a plug hat is like a red rag to a bull. When I was a kid—"

"Bet you a quarter I can knock it off first," said Bill, picking up a rock.

"Your first shot," said Wes.

But just as Bill raised his arm, he dropped it again and said: "Hey!" in a startled voice. For Eek and Quik and Eeny and Cousin Augustus had jumped off the hat brim into the grass.

"Looked like mice," said Wes. "What do you suppose—"

"Let's go over and see," said Bill.

Freddy knew that something had to be done, and done quickly. So all at once he dropped his arms. "Don't you come over here!" he shouted. "Don't you come near this place."

"Doggone!" said Bill. "It's alive!"

"Who are you, and what are you doing there?" demanded Wes in his most official voice.

"I'm out here makin' my livin', that's what I'm doing," said Freddy angrily, "and what business is it of policemen to throw rocks at me, I should like to know. Going about my lawful business, I am, and it's your duty to protect me, not throw things at me. Wait until I report this to your commanding officer, my lads, and see what *he* says."

The troopers glanced at each other. After all,

throwing stones, even at a scarecrow, wasn't part of their duty, and if they were throwing them at a man, and the matter was reported to the lieutenant—well, it wouldn't be any help towards promotion.

"We're sorry," said Bill. "We thought you were a scarecrow."

"A scarecrow!" yelled Freddy. "Me—a scarecrow? By George, young man, I'll see you punished for that kind of insulting talk if I have to carry the matter to Albany. Fine guardians of the peace, you are! Calling names; throwing rocks—"

"Excuse me, mister," said Wes. "We really didn't mean anything against you. But you were standing out there with your arms apart, and not moving—"

"*Course* I'm not moving," said the pig. "How can I catch 'em if I move?"

"Catch what?" asked Bill.

"Mice. I'm a professional catcher and trainer of mice. Put crumbs on my hat, come out and stand still, mice get on hat for crumbs, I scoop 'em into my pocket, take 'em home and train 'em. Anything illegal about that?"

"No, no," said Bill soothingly. "It's a new occupation to me, but as far as I can see, no harm in it if you like it."

"And I hope," said Wes, "that you'll reconsider about reporting us. A report like that—"

"I can tell you one thing, my lad," said Freddy; "you'll be reported if you give me any more of your talk. Get along, and we'll say no more about it. But keep this up another minute or two—" The balance of his remarks was lost in the roar of the motorcycles as the troopers kicked them into action.

"Wow!" said Freddy. "Now I *have* got to sit down and cool off!"

Chapter 10

The tents of Boomschmidt's Colossal and Unparalleled Circus had been pitched in the fair grounds just west of the village of South Pharisee. Freddy and Jinx saw the flags flying a long way off, and then as they came closer they saw the big tent with the little tents around it, and the red and gold wagons, and the crowds of people. They went up to the gate where, in a little booth, an ostrich was taking tickets.

There was one thing about Mr. Boomschmidt's circus that was different from every other circus, and that was that the animals weren't kept locked up in their cages, but were allowed to mingle with the customers, and even did a good deal of the work usually done by attendants. Naturally at first people were inclined to be a little nervous when they were shown to their seats by a hippopotamus, or when they went into a sideshow and found a full grown tiger looking over their shoulder. But as the Boomschmidt show came back to the same towns year after year, they got used to it and began to like it. And when mothers saw their children being chased by a leopard or a hyena, they didn't scream and carry on, but just smiled happily and said: "What fun they have, to be sure!" It was a very good arrangement all around.

Freddy and Jinx got in line and moved up to the gate.

"Hello, Oscar. How are you?" said Freddy.

But the ostrich just looked at him and said: "Tickets, please."

Freddy took off his hat. "Remember me now? I'm—"

"If you haven't tickets," said the ostrich in a snippy voice, "kindly stand to one side."

Some of the people giggled, and a woman behind Freddy said: "Oh, move on; we can't stand here all day!"

"But I want to see Mr. Boomschmidt," Freddy persisted. "I'm a friend of his. I'm Freddy, the pig that—"

"I see you're a pig," said Oscar, "but Mr. Boomschmidt isn't hiring any more talent. We have all the trained animals we need for the show. Now kindly step aside or I shall have to use force."

Freddy was a good deal embarrassed at being obliged to hold up the line, and he was about to step aside and try one of the other entrances, when Jinx, who had been getting madder and madder, suddenly stuck his face into the ticket window.

"Oh," he said, "so you want to pretend you don't remember us, hey? Well, it's all right with us. Why anybody'd want to know an overgrown biped with his knees turned backwards and a length of garden hose for a neck I don't know. But you let us in to the boss, or I'll come through this window and take those plumes of yours to trim my friend's hat!"

"Well, really!" said the ostrich, and he started out of the booth.

"Come on," said Freddy, taking hold of Jinx' paw. For an ostrich can kick as hard as a mule. But at that moment a large lion came bounding up.

"What's going on here?" he demanded.

"These—these persons," said Oscar, "are trying to force their way in without tickets. I was about to—"

"Well, dye my hair!" roared the lion suddenly. "It's Freddy and Jinx! Why this makes the day perfect!" And he put his paws around Freddy's neck and hugged him.

Then he pushed the pig back and looked at him. "What makes you squeak like that?"

" 'Tisn't me," said Freddy, picking up the hat which had fallen off; "it's the mice in my pockets. You were suffocating them."

"Oh, sorry," said the lion. "Hello, boys," he said to the mice, who stuck their heads out and waved to him. "And Jinx," he added, shaking hands with the cat. "My, won't the boss be glad

"Well, dye my hair!"

to see you!" He turned to Oscar. "No tickets, hey, you ninny? Of course they haven't tickets. You know them as well as I do, and you know we wouldn't take tickets from them if they had them. You ought to be ashamed, ostrich. You're getting so stuck up that sometimes I wonder if you'll even talk to yourself!

"I'm glad you've come," the lion said as he led them across towards the big tent. "The boss is kind of low, and maybe you can cheer him up. Attendance hasn't been nearly as good as usual this year, and he was planning to pep it up with a balloon ascension, but the fellow lost his balloon. Can you beat it? I should think a balloon would be about the last thing anybody could lose."

"That's partly what I want to see him about," said Freddy. "I think I can fix that up."

"Trust you," said the lion. "I bet you've got something up your sleeve. Something besides mice, that is," he added, nudging the pig in the ribs.

They found Mr. Boomschmidt out back of the big tent, inspecting what appeared to be a huge cannon. He was a short round man in a suit of large bright checks and a silk hat, which he wore on the back of his head.

"Hey, chief! Company!" called the lion.

Mr. Boomschmidt looked up, and then hurried over to meet them with his hand outstretched. "Jinx!" he exclaimed. "Well, this *is* a pleasure! And this other gentleman— No, no, don't tell me. Why, upon my soul! It's Freddy. In disguise, of course. Detecting somebody, I suppose. Well, I should never have known you, Freddy."

"You did know him though, chief," said the lion.

"Eh?" said Mr. Boomschmidt. "Of course I knew him. What I meant was: if I hadn't, I wouldn't have. Don't be so technical, Leo. My goodness, you two have come at just the right moment. Tell them that they have come at just the right moment, Leo."

"The boss means that maybe you can think of something to do with this cannon," said Leo. "We got it a couple of years ago, and every performance Bill Wonks used to get into it and be shot out into a net. But last Thursday when the boss loaded it, he got too much powder in, and it shot Bill right over the big tent and into the window of a house across the road. There was a woman doing her washing in the house, and Bill landed in a tub of hot suds. He was kind of mad about it."

"I don't exactly blame him," said Jinx.

"He was clean for once, anyway," said Leo. "But he won't do it any more, and we can't get any more volunteers."

"Why do you have to shoot anybody out of the gun?" asked Freddy. "You've got a good enough show without that."

"That's just the point," said Mr. Boom-schmidt. "You see, our show is mostly animal acts, but animal acts isn't enough. We've got to have at least one act that is dangerous—or at least looks that way. I don't know why it is, but if folks think somebody's maybe going to get chewed up by a lion or fall off a trapeze and break his leg, they'll fill every seat in the big tent. My goodness, why is that, Leo? No, never mind; don't tell me; I want to finish what I was saying. Oh dear, where was I?"

"You have to have one dangerous act," prompted Jinx.

"Oh yes, of course. Well, you see, we can't make our lion taming act, for instance, look dangerous, because no matter how much Leo here roars, he can't scare folks that call him by his first name and maybe had him over to supper the night before. So that's why we got the gun."

"They have to call me by my first name," put in Leo, "because that's all I've got."

"My goodness, so it is!" said Mr. Boomschmidt. "Why Leo, why did I never think of that before? We must get a last name for you right away. It's a dreadful oversight. How could people write letters to you, or—" He stopped. "There, now I've lost my place again," he said.

"I wish you wouldn't keep getting me off the track, Leo." He pushed his hat back and scratched the front of his head thoughtfully, and then he pushed the hat forward and scratched the back of his head, and then he said: "Oh, yes; the gun, wasn't it? Well, when Bill struck, I had to find something else to look dangerous, and I hired a man named Golcher to go up in a balloon. But my goodness, then it turns out he hasn't a balloon. So then I tried to get some volunteers to be shot out of the gun. And that was a funny thing, and I don't know quite how to explain it: we had nine volunteers, but every one of them was an elephant or a rhino or some animal too big to go into the gun at all. And none of the animals who were small enough volunteered at all. My goodness, how do you explain that? Are big animals braver than little animals, or—"

"I can explain it, chief," said Leo.

"Well, don't. You'll get me off again, and I want to finish. Now where was . . . Oh, yes. Well, I did get some small volunteers. Five young blackbirds. I hired 'em and we had all the arrangements made. We were going to shoot 'em into that big tree over there. Load 'em into the gun, point it at that empty tree, bang!—tree's full of birds. Instead of shooting birds *out* of trees, we'd shoot 'em *into* trees. Wasn't that a good idea? Eh, Leo, you tell 'em what a good idea it was."

"You tell 'em, boss," said the lion. "It was your idea."

"Well," said Mr. Boomschmidt, "it was, anyway. But just as we were all ready, the birds' mother came over, and my, my, what a rumpus she made about it! She said I had no business to hire young innocent birds hardly out of the nest for such dangerous work, and she said she was going to have the law on me because they were miners." He stopped and thought a minute. "Now that was a funny thing to say, wasn't it? I never thought of that until this minute. Miners, indeed! I guess I know a miner when I see one. He has a little lamp in his hat and a pickaxe and a dirty face. Now what did she mean—"

"She meant 'minors,' chief. With an o. Meaning they were too young to work."

"With an o?" said Mr. Boomschmidt. "Oh. —That is, I mean: Oh, exclamation point. Why yes, of course. Well, I'm glad to have that cleared up. It bothered me. But anyway, then we couldn't use 'em, could we, Leo? So there we were. I don't suppose either of you two would like to be shot out of a gun?"

"No," said Jinx and Freddy together.

"Well, I thought maybe you wouldn't. Dear me, it's very annoying. If that man Golcher hadn't gone and lost his balloon. Said a pig stole it—can you imagine that? I can't. Even Leo can't, and he's got a wonderful imagination."

"Yes I can too, chief," said Leo. "You remember Golcher said it was a special kind of pig?"

"My goodness, of course I remember. He said it was a *talking* pig. He said it . . . came . . . from . . ." Mr. Boomschmidt's mouth stayed open, although his voice stopped coming out of it as he stared at Freddy, and then suddenly he said in a loud voice: "No!"

Freddy nodded. "Yes," he said, "it was me. But I didn't steal it."

"Maybe you didn't," said Mr. Boomschmidt, "but if the police catch you you'll have a hard time proving it."

"That's why I came to see you," said Freddy, and he told them about his adventure, and about the two hundred dollars that Mr. Bean had paid Mr. Golcher. "Now," he said, "if I could get the balloon over here in time for Mr. Golcher to go up in it tomorrow, you'd pay him his two hundred for it, and he would give back Mr. Bean's two hundred, and everybody would be satisfied. I don't believe he'd keep on trying to have me arrested after that."

Mr. Boomschmidt thought that would work all right, but how was Freddy to get the balloon over to South Pharisee?

"I thought maybe you'd lend me a couple of the elephants, and we could go over for it after dark, and they could tow it back."

"Why, we'd be glad to, Freddy. Wouldn't we, Leo? I don't usually like to have the elephants on the road after dark, because they're so careless about remembering to carry lights. The last time Louise was out at night, a big truck ran into her."

"Was she badly hurt?" asked Jinx.

"Oh, it didn't hurt Louise, but it broke one of the truck wheels and I had to pay for it. But if you see that they keep their lights on, it'll be all right."

"Look, boss," said Leo. "Golcher's around somewhere. Suppose I go and see if he'll agree to this."

"Don't tell him I'm here," said Freddy. "Oh, and there's another thing: you can tell him that as an added feature to make the ascension a success, I can lend him four mice who are parachute jumpers. I brought them along because I thought he'd like the idea."

"You leave it to me," said the lion. "And, boss," he added; "you'll have to get out of here. The evening show's going to start, and you have to lead the parade."

Jinx and the mice thought they would go in and see the show, but Freddy felt that he ought to keep out of sight until things were settled, so Mr. Boomschmidt took him into his private office. This was just one of the houses on wheels that the circus people lived in, and all it contained was a very large and comfortable bed in which Mr. Boomschmidt slept, and a very small and uncomfortable chair before the desk at which Mr. Boomschmidt worked. The chair didn't look as if it was used very much. At one end of the room was an oil painting of Mr. Boomschmidt's mother, and at the other end, an oil painting of Mr. Boomschmidt himself. Except that Mr. Boomschmidt had on a silk hat and Mrs. Boomschmidt had on a bonnet, you couldn't tell them apart.

Freddy was pretty tired after his long hot walk, and so he took off his silk hat and lay down on the bed, and Mr. Boomschmidt covered him up with an afghan. Over in the big tent he could hear the hurrahs and the hand-clapping, and the *ta-ra, ra-ra, oompah, oompah* of the band. It was all very pleasantly far away and soothing . . . and the next thing he knew, somebody was shaking his shoulder and Leo's voice was saying: "Hey, Freddy, wake up! You've got to get out of here!"

Chapter 11

Freddy made one bound off the bed and into the middle of the floor, as if he had been set on springs. "Don't you touch me!" he said. "I didn't do it. I didn't have anything to do with it. Send for my lawyer. Send for Mr. Bean. Send for— Oh," he said, sinking down into the chair, "it's you, Leo!"

"My! my! You certainly come out fighting, Freddy," said the lion.

"Dreamt somebody stole the dome off the

Capitol at Washington, and the police arrested me for it," said the pig.

"Well, you better dream some more. You don't gain much by waking up. Because old Golcher is going to send for the police and have them search the circus grounds for you."

"You mean—you mean he wouldn't play ball with us?"

"No. I made him your proposition, and at first I thought everything was all right, because he said if you got the balloon back in time for you to go up tomorrow, he'd tell the police you didn't steal it. But when I said of course he'd give the two hundred back to Mr. Bean, he said: 'Of course, nothing! Bean didn't pay me to make an ascension.'

" 'He paid you what you thought you'd lost by not being able to make it,' I said.

"But he didn't see it that way. The two hundred Mr. Bean paid him, he said, was for—how was it?—'mental anguish and laceration of feelings,'—that was it. Meaning, I suppose, the worry he had over thinking the balloon was lost. Anyway, he's going to keep both two hundreds.

"Well I said to him—I said: 'Some folks would call that dishonest, Mr. Golcher.' He just laughed. 'Golcher dishonest?' he said. 'Well, now, that's a matter of opinion, and such opinions are usually settled in a court of law. If Mr. Bean, or that smart pig, thinks I'm dishonest, why all they got to do is argue it out before a judge and jury. 'Tain't any good talking about dishonesty; you got to prove it, or it isn't so.'"

"We couldn't go to law about it," said Freddy. "It's too complicated a case, and besides, I'd be in jail."

"You'll be in jail anyway if you don't get away from here," said Leo. "Because after I'd argued with him for a while, he said: 'Say, you seem to know a lot about this pig; where is he?' and I said: 'Wouldn't you like to know?' and he said: 'I would, and I think I'll have the police come search the circus and find out.'"

"Pooh," said Freddy, "they'd never recognize me in this disguise."

"Yeah? Well, listen to this. You remember Leslie?—he's that young alligator that can turn cartwheels—well, he hangs out down at state police headquarters a lot, because he likes to play checkers. He's good at it, too. Well, he just got back in time for his act, and he told me before he went on that the police got a complaint from a farmer that his scarecrow's clothes had been stolen.''

"Oh," said Freddy. "So they'll be looking for somebody in those clothes?"

"Worse than that. Wes and Bill remembered that they'd seen clothes like that twice, and they put two and two together and decided that the scarecrow and the mouse trainer were the same person, and that they were probably a pig named Freddy who stole a balloon. Because, they said, why look for two thieves when one will do?"

"Oh, golly," said Freddy wearily. "I ought to beat it right now, but I can't go with a disguise and I certainly can't go without one. If I could get to that balloon, I guess I'd just like to sail off into the sky and never be heard of again."

"Well, dye my hair!" exclaimed Leo perplexedly. "I never thought to hear you give up as easy as that. Just because the cops are beginning to close in on you. A pig that's done what you've done and seen what you've seen. Why, you haven't even *begun* to fight, Freddy."

"Eh?" said Freddy. "Maybe you're right." He frowned. At first his frown was thoughtful, but gradually it grew fierce. "You *are* right!" he said, and began stripping off the scarecrow's clothes. "I'm not licked yet—not by a long shot. I'm going out there, just like this, a pig and proud of it, and let 'em come take me if they can! Just let 'em try it! Just—"

"Hey, hold on," said the lion; "you can't fight the whole police force. You certainly do change quick."

"I expect it's my poetic temperament," said Freddy, "always flying from one extreme to the other. But I suppose you're right. Fighting's no good; we've got to use guile."

"Is that some kind of disguise?" inquired the lion.

Freddy was about to explain, when there was a tap at the door. Leo motioned him to stay out of sight, and opened the door a crack. "Oh, it's only you, Abdullah," and he opened the door wider. "Come in."

The man who came in was very dark, and he

had a big turban on his head and wore a white robe. He was one of the elephant drivers, and his name was really Ed Peabody, but he was called Abdullah and dressed like an East Indian because he had to ride on the head of Hannibal, the biggest elephant, in the parade.

"Why aren't you with Hannibal?" asked Leo. "The elephant act will go on in a few minutes."

"I came over to tell the boss," said Abdullah. "I can't go on with 'em tonight. I feel all sort of sick and dizzy."

"You've been eating Hannibal's peanuts again," said Leo.

"Well, I can't help it," said Abdullah. "The kids give 'em to him, and you know Mr. Boomschmidt says they aren't good for him and I mustn't let him eat them. And my old mother always said: Never throw away good food. So—"

"All right, all right," said Leo. "Tell that to the chief, not to me. But somebody's got to ride Hannibal . . . Hey, wait a minute!" he exclaimed. "This will fix the whole thing. Give your turban and robe to Freddy, Abdullah. He'll take your place. Look, Freddy: if there's once place the cops won't expect to find you, it's on top of an elephant. Then when the show's over, and it's dark, you can go with Hannibal and Louise for the balloon." He looked sharply at the pig. "Only we'll have to put something on your face to darken it. Gracious, I never realized how blonde pigs were. I'll touch you up with some of Bill Wonks' hair dye, that he uses on his moustache."

"Well, dye my face!" murmured Freddy unhappily.

And so when the animals marched into the big tent to go through their drill and do all their tricks, it was Freddy, in robe and turban, and with a complexion as swarthy as a Moor's, who sat cross-legged on the back of Hannibal's neck and bowed graciously right and left to the thunder of applause. And it was Freddy who giggled so that he nearly fell off when, as he marched by one of the front benches, he saw Jinx and the four mice clapping their paws enthusiastically. "Wait until they know who they've been applauding!" he said to himself.

But his thoughts took a more solemn turn when a few minutes later he saw four state troopers walking down past the benches in dif-

. . . it was Freddy, in robe and turban.

ferent parts of the tent, and looking closely at the audience. As the elephants went through their routine, he kept his eye on the troopers. Here and there one of them would tap a man on the shoulder, and he and the man would exchange a few words, and then the trooper would go on. Gradually the audience became aware of this activity, and some were annoyed by it, and some were scared, and pretty soon everybody was watching the troopers and nobody was watching the elephants, or even the clowns.

So then Mr. Boomschmidt stepped out into the middle of the ring and held up his hands. "La-dees and gentlemen," he shouted; "it has perhaps not escaped your attention that for the past fifteen minutes two shows have been going on under this tent. There is the show provided at great expense for your amusement by Boomschmidt's Colossal and Unparalleled Circus, and there is the show provided, as far as I can see to no purpose and at no expense at all, by the gentlemen of the police. Since Boomschmidt's Colossal and Unparalleled Circus does not believe in arguing with the police, the animals and clowns of Boomschmidt's Colossal and Unparalleled Circus will now withdraw, and permit the police to continue with their own performance uninterrupted."

"No, no!" shouted the audience. "Go on with the show. Throw the police out."

"Perhaps, then," said Mr. Boomschmidt, "the police will tell us what they are looking for, and we can help them find it, and go on with the show."

"We're looking for a pig who stole a balloon," called Bill from the top row of seats. "We have information that he is in this tent."

At this news that they were suspected of being a pig, some of the people who had been questioned by the police began to talk angrily to their neighbors, and others turned and looked suspiciously at people beside them or behind them, and the ones looked at got mad and several fights started. Down in the front row an old gentleman who had on the only silk hat in the audience turned on the trooper who had been questioning him. "Look like a pig, do I? I'll have you know I'm Henry P. Utterly, senior partner in the law firm of Utterly, Utterly, Wimpole and Winker, and I shall start suit against you at once for defamation of character, malfeasance in office, and skulduggery in the first degree, and your case will be tried before Judge Utterly, which is me, and how do you like that, young man?"

"Oh, gosh!" said the trooper unhappily.

"La-dees and gentlemen!" shouted Mr. Boomschmidt again. "The opinion expressed by the police that any one of this distinguished audience resembles a pig is one which you very naturally resent. Not that I have anything against pigs—my goodness, no. As a lifelong friend and companion of animals, I count among my most cherished friends members of the porcine race. And a pig—*as* pig—can be a very handsome animal. I should be the last to deny it.

"On the other hand, a pig looks like a pig, and a man looks like a man. No pig wants to look like a man, and—per contra, conversely, and vice versa—no man wants to be told that he looks like a pig. Therefore, ladies and gentlemen, I suggest to the respected gentlemen of the police that more harm will be done by a continuation of their search here than by the possible escape of this pig. Particularly since the pig is known to me personally as a thoroughly honest, reliable and talented animal, who I don't for a moment believe ever stole so much as a pin from anybody."

There were loud cheers from the audience, and even from the elephants, for it was felt that Mr. Boomschmidt had dealt firmly and tactfully with a difficult situation. Freddy could hardly restrain himself from jumping down and going over to thank his friend, particularly when he knew that his appearance at that moment would be received with the most enthusiastic applause. But he held himself back. And the troopers withdrew and the show went on. And then, as soon as it was over, Freddy and Louise and Hannibal set out to find the balloon.

Chapter 12

After Freddy had left them, the two ducks tidied up the balloon basket. They folded the blankets and ponchos, and repacked the hamper and the box of canned goods, and dusted and picked up so that everything was as neat as a pin. And then they sat on the edge of the basket and rested, and if they had had rocking chairs, I guess they would have rocked.

"Well, sister," said Alice, "if anyone had ever told us that we would actually have enjoyed such a dangerous trip, we wouldn't have believed them, would we?"

"Dear me," said Emma, "have we enjoyed it? Why, I suppose we have. My, my, how proud Uncle Wesley would have been of us!"

"He would indeed. And how he would have enjoyed it here. Why, it's as if we had our own front porch to sit on." Then Alice frowned thoughtfully and looked at her sister. "Did it occur to you, Emma, that something that eagle said might have referred to Uncle Wesley?

Maybe you have never seen a duck frown thoughtfully. To tell the truth, I never have. But I do not see why, with practice, a highly educated duck like Alice couldn't do it; and anyway, I am reliably informed that she did.

Emma gave her a startled look. "You mean—you mean what he said about the farm at South Pharisee?—when they thought we weren't listening? It did indeed occur to me. But I didn't say anything about it because neither Freddy nor Breckenridge seemed to want us to overhear it."

Alice nodded her head. "We were always taught," she said, "that when you overhear a conversation that is not meant for your ears, you should try at once to forget it. But in this case I think perhaps we are carrying good manners too far. Let us now admit that we heard it."

"Well . . . I admit it," said Emma.

"So did I. And if it is true, as Breckenridge seemed to hint, that Uncle Wesley is living on such a farm, then I think we should do something about it."

"But what can we do?"

"I don't know," said Alice. "Let me think." And she closed her eyes as she had seen Freddy do when he was thinking. But in a minute she opened them again. "I must say," she said, "I don't see how Freddy manages it."

"Manages what?"

"Thinking with his eyes shut. Goodness, I should go right to sleep."

"So does Freddy, I fancy," said Emma. "Only he pretends he's awake all the time."

"He does think of things, though."

"Perhaps they come to him in his sleep," said Emma. "Why don't you try it?"

So Alice shut her eyes and put her head under her wing, and Emma watched her anxiously.

Emma didn't try it herself, because she never thought of anything anyway, whether she was awake or asleep. She always said that it was no use her trying to think—it just confused her.

After quite a long time Alice took her head out from under her wing.

"Did you think of anything?" Emma asked.

"No," said Alice disgustedly. "I just dreamt that we jumped out of the basket. We spread our wings and fluttered down. Why, dear me," she said in a surprised voice, "I suppose I did think of something. We can jump down and go see if Uncle Wesley is on that farm. Only it does seem to me that I could have thought of that without going to sleep."

Emma said in a weak voice that perhaps if she went to sleep again she'd think of something better, but Alice retorted that whatever they decided to do, they'd have to get out of the balloon first, and jumping was the only way. "If you're afraid," she said, "I'll go, and you can wait here."

Emma sidled to the edge and peered over, and she shuddered so hard that a feather flew out of her wing and went floating slowly earthward. And then suddenly her foot slipped, and with a loud quack of terror she fell.

"Oh, preserve us all!" exclaimed Alice, and craned her neck out over the edge, half expecting to see fragments of Emma strewn over the ground below. What she did see was quite different. For Emma had spread her wings and was beating the air to keep from falling. Indeed she fluttered so frantically, that for a second or two she stayed motionless in the air. And her fear suddenly left her.

"Look, sister, look!" she called, and began giggling delightedly. "I'm—tee, hee—I'm flying! I'm cutting regular—hee, hee, hee!—regular capers!" And indeed she did almost succeed in turning a back flip before her unaccustomed wings began to get tired, and she stopped fluttering, and with wings spread, glided down in a long slow curve to the ground.

"Oh, try it, sister," she called up. "It's quite delightful. And so easy! Why, I had no idea!"

"Well," said Alice doubtfully, and then she clamped her bill tight shut and jumped.

Down on the ground, both ducks were so pleased with their experience that they would have liked to do it over again. But there was no way of getting back into the basket.

"We'll have to go to South Pharisee now," said Alice. "Oh, Mr. Webb!" she called, and when the spider came sliding down a long strand of cobweb below the basket, she told him where they were going. "We'll try to get back before Freddy does," she said, and Mr. Webb waved some of his legs to show that he understood.

Ducks aren't built for woods travel, and the sisters had a hard time of it until they came out on a road that they had seen earlier from the balloon. They waddled down this for half a mile or so, and then struck the main road, and there was a sign that said: South Pharisee, 6 Miles.

Emma sighed. "I'll never make it," she said. "Never in the world."

"Perhaps we can thumb a ride," said Alice.

"We haven't any thumbs."

"Well, we can only try," said Alice, and as a car whirled by she waved one wing in the direction they were going, and quacked as loud as she could. But the man in the car glanced at them and said briefly: "Ducks," and his wife said:

"Uh-huh," and they went right on.

After several cars had done this, they decided it was no use and they'd better walk. So they started on. Pretty soon they met a squirrel. He was sitting on the stone wall beside the road examining a last year's hickory nut.

"Excuse me, sir," said Alice, "but can you tell us where the Pratt farm is?"

"Which one?" said the squirrel. "There's Adam Pratt up towards Newcome, and there's Ezekiel Pratt up on Lost Creek, and there's Hiram Pratt—"

"We want the one that lives near South Pharisee," interrupted Alice.

The squirrel gnawed at the nut a minute, and then he said: "They all live near South Pharisee. There's Zebediah Pratt at Winkville, and there's Zenas Pratt on the Corntassel Road, and—"

"Oh, wait a minute, please," said Alice. "We're looking for my uncle, and—"

"If your uncle's one of the Pratts, you ought to know his first name," said the squirrel.

"He isn't one of the Pratts," replied Alice, "and if you'd listen a minute I could tell you.

He's a duck, and he lives on a farm owned by a Mr. Pratt."

"A duck," said the squirrel. "I suppose I should have guessed it. You don't favor the Pratts. All dark-complected folks, the Pratts are." He went on gnawing for a minute, and then he said: "All the Pratts keep ducks."

"Oh, dear!" said Emma, and Alice started to ask the squirrel something, when all at once he began to jump up and down angrily. He had gnawed through the shell of the nut and tasted the kernel. "Just as I thought!" he chattered. "Another rotten one!" Then he looked down at them. "Ducks!" he exclaimed contemptuously. "Pah!" And he threw the nut at Alice.

"Well, really!" said Emma, and Alice said: "There's no excuse for bad manners, young man. If you can't be civil—"

"Well, I can't," said the squirrel. "Not with ducks. Not today, anyway. You wait till I get my paws on that Wesley! I'll show *him*!"

"Wesley!" exclaimed Emma. "Why, that's our uncle's name! Oh, where is he?"

The squirrel scratched his head. "*Your* uncle? Why, he could be, at that. What does he look like—something like this?" And he stuck out his chest, pulled in his chin, and stared down his nose importantly at them.

"Why, he—he does look a little . . . Only of course you're making fun of him. He has a sort of bold, fearless look."

"You wait till I get hold of him and see what happens to his bold fearless look. That's the sixth rotten nut he's sold me this week."

"Sold you?" said Alice. "I don't think I understand."

"You mean that Uncle Wesley is in *trade?*" exclaimed Alice.

"Not much of a trade for me," said the squirrel. "All those good bread crusts I brought him."

"Bread crusts, sister," said Emma. "You remember how fond he always was of bread crusts, and Mrs. Bean used to save them for him, because Mr. Bean wouldn't eat the crust of store bread?"

"Yes, it must be he," said Alice. "Will you take us to him, sir?"

"You come with me," said the squirrel, looking very determined. "Because I'm going to pick a bone with Wesley, and the only thing I haven't decided is which bone it'll be. Except it won't be one of mine."

"You'd better be careful," said Emma. "Uncle Wesley won't stand any nonsense. He simply doesn't know the meaning of fear."

"He will before suppertime," said the squirrel, and he started off along the wall.

"Just a minute," said Alice. "If this really is our Uncle Wesley—and it certainly sounds like him—I am going to give you a word of advice, young man. If you have a complaint, I'm sure he'll listen to it. He's very fair. But don't say anything to provoke his anger. He is really terrible when he's angry."

"He's pretty terrible any way you look at him," said the squirrel with a grin. "Well, come on if you want to."

The ducks shook their heads doubtfully at the squirrel's temerity, but they followed him up the road a quarter of a mile, then through a fence and across two fields to a little stream that ran down into a patch of woods. And on the way he told them about the hermit duck named Wesley, who lived all alone in these woods, which were on the Hiram Pratt farm. Even the squirrels, who always know everything that is going on, didn't know where he came from or why he lived alone. "I found out he liked bread crusts, so every now and then I take him down some and trade them for nuts he's picked up in the woods. But I've got to quit it. Six out of the last dozen rotten! That's too much of a good thing." He stopped on the bank of the stream at the edge of the woods. "Well, here we are. Maybe you'd better call him, one of you."

"Afraid?" asked Alice contemptuously.

"Afraid he won't come out if he knows I'm here—sure," said the squirrel.

"He'll come out all right, if he's our uncle," said Alice. And as the ducks refused to call him, the squirrel said oh, very well, he'd try it.

"We'll hide," said Alice. "Because we know Uncle Wesley would always be polite in front of ladies, and we don't specially want him to be polite to you—not after the things you've said about him."

"Oh, Wesley! Where are you, old chap?" called the squirrel.

Alice nudged her sister happily. "What a surprise *he'll* get if he says anything insulting to Uncle Wesley!"

"I'm sort of sorry for that poor squirrel," said Emma. "He doesn't know."

There was a rustling in the bushes, and in a minute a pompous little white duck waddled out. It was Uncle Wesley all right.

"Well, well, Rudy; how are you today?" he said. "More bread crusts to trade? I'm sorry we're all out of hickory nuts, but we have some very nice acorns this morning."

"Acorns!" shouted the squirrel. "Nice rotten acorns, and dried up hickory nuts—that's the kind of stuff you've been trading me. Six rotten in the last dozen, and you'll make 'em good, and right now, or you've quacked your last quack."

"Now, now—easy, young man," said Uncle Wesley, backing away. "Certainly I'll make good anything that is not wholly satisfactory. No cause for all this uproar."

"All right, roll 'em out!" demanded the squirrel. "Six of 'em, and make it snappy, you robber."

"Yes, yes; don't be impatient," quacked Uncle Wesley. "There'll be a little delay, I'm afraid. We haven't at the moment any really first class nuts in stock, but if you can come back in two days—"

Alice and Emma stared at each other in consternation. "But that *can't* be our Uncle Wesley!" said Emma. "Why he wouldn't let a *lion* talk to him like that!"

The argument went on, with the squirrel talking louder and louder, and Uncle Wesley backing farther and farther away, until at last the squirrel suddenly lost all control of himself, and leaping at the duck, gave him a push that sent him fluttering and protesting over the bank into the water.

"Come, come—this is too much!" said Alice and Emma, and they rushed out from their hiding place and flew at the squirrel, striking him with their wings and bills until they had driven him over the bank after their uncle. Then they stood over him menacingly as he crawled out, dripping and gasping, while Uncle Wesley watched prudently from the other side of the stream.

"You'd better go home, since you don't seem

"All right, roll 'em out!"

to know how to act like a gentleman," said Alice severely.

"I want those nuts," replied the squirrel, beginning to cry.

"Our Uncle Wesley is not a robber," said Emma. "He will give you the nuts if he owes them to you. Uncle Wesley," she called, "can't you settle this matter?"

"Why, my dear nieces!" exclaimed the duck. "What a pleasure! And what a surprise! Of course, of course. One moment." And he disappeared.

A few minutes later he returned with six nuts wrapped in a large leaf, and when the squirrel had gone off home with them, still sniffling, he said:

"Well, well, my dears; how on earth did you find me? And what brings you here?"

"We'll tell you about that later," said Alice. "Right now, we'd like you to start back home with us. We've missed you, Uncle Wesley. The pond hasn't seemed the same since you went away. Why did you stay here all these years?"

"Dear, dear; the old pond!" said Uncle Wesley sentimentally. "Well, it's a long story. I should like to tell it to you. Can you stay a few days with me in my modest forest retreat?"

"We would love to," said Alice, "but we really have to leave very soon."

"Well, do sit down for a little while," said Uncle Wesley. "There is a little backwater in the brook here that is quite cool and comfortable. I hope you won't rush right off again. Dear me," he said, shaking his head, "I hope that squirrel's impudence didn't upset you. Perhaps I was too patient with his nonsense. I should have thrown him into the brook at once, instead of listening to him until he became violent. But I never like to use force against smaller animals."

"But—but *we* were the ones that threw him in the brook, Uncle Wesley," said Emma.

"Ah, yes; so you were, my dear." He shook his head again. "Tut, tut; I'm afraid you rather forgot yourselves there. I don't like to scold you the very first thing after such a long separation, but it was hardly ladylike, was it? I do hope that in my absence you haven't forgotten your manners. —However, let us say no more about it now. How are you both?"

The sisters looked at each other. This was the Uncle Wesley that they knew and admired. But why had he acted in such a cowardly way with the squirrel? They were pretty puzzled. But they said that they were well, and after giving him the news of the farm, and telling him about their trip, they again repeated their wish that he should go back home with them. "We had an idea," said Alice, "that when you left us so suddenly, you went unwillingly. You said nothing to us; one morning you were just gone. We were dreadfully worried."

"I knew that you must be," said Uncle Wesley. "But there was no way to let you know. You see, I had gone out for my morning walk when I was attacked by an eagle. No doubt he mistook me for some simple domestic fowl who could offer no resistance." Uncle Wesley laughed. "How surprised that eagle was when he found out who he had really tackled! I fancy I put up rather more of a fight than he expected. Of course, his superior weight and strength were in his favor, but courage and skill will always win in the end, and it was no different in this case. I beat him severely, and at last he gave in and flew off screaming. But he had carried me up into the air, and the fight went on for a good many miles, so that when I came to earth I was in entirely strange country. Well, there was no question of trying to get home, for I had sprained my ankle in landing. So in looking around for a place to stay, I found this delightful spot. I quite fell in love with it. So much pleasanter than the Bean farm, with all those great animals tramping around and getting in the way! Don't you agree?"

"Why, it's very pleasant," said Emma. "But do you mean that you really didn't want to come back home?"

"Want to? Of course I wanted to. But you know how it is. You stay on from day to day, always saying: 'Well, tomorrow I'll start home.' But I would hardly expect you to understand, my dears. You have led such a sheltered and protected life; the very thought of travel and adventure is terrifying to you. But in me there is a strong strain of the adventurer, the gypsy. Ah, adventure, the open road, the thrill of danger—!"

"This doesn't seem very adventurous to me,"

said Alice flatly. "Living in a safe little hideout in the woods."

"And I guess we haven't been so terrified as you think," said Emma. "We thought you'd be very pleased, Uncle Wesley, at our taking this trip."

"Come, come, my dears," said the duck severely. "You mustn't argue with your old uncle. I'm afraid that in my long absence you have allowed yourselves to become a little unladylike. But there; we will soon correct that. For you must give up this nonsense about going back to the Bean farm, which I always disliked. You will from now on live here with me."

Alice took a deep breath and let it out again without saying anything; then she took another, and this time she said: "We want you to go home with us."

"Sister!" exclaimed Emma in dismay, and Uncle Wesley puffed out his chest and pulled in his chin and stared at her. But for the first time in her life Alice stared back. "See here, Uncle Wesley," she said; "maybe we have changed since you went away, but I can tell you we've changed more in the past ten minutes than in

all the rest of the time. But never mind that
now. We have always admired you intensely,
and have done always what we thought would
please you. You told us that we were poor weak
females whom it was your duty to guard from
danger and unpleasantness. You, on the other
hand, you said, were bold and adventurous by
nature. Well, we would like to continue to
think that you are. We'd like to think that it was
your example that made us go on this balloon
trip. But we can't think so if you refuse an adventure that two poor weak females aren't
afraid of. Do you agree, sister?"

Emma looked doubtfully at her uncle. "Oh,
forgive me, Uncle Wesley, but I—I'm afraid I
do."

Uncle Wesley stared at them a moment, then
turned his back, and bowing his head: "That I
should live to see the day," he said mournfully,
"when my own nieces, whom I have nurtured
in every luxury—"

"Boloney!" said a loud voice in the treetops
above them, and they looked up to see the squirrel staring down at them.

"Give it to him, girls," said the squirrel. "I

know his kind. Regular tyrant around the house with his women folks, but as meek as Moses out around town. Made you toe the mark, I bet. Told you he was as brave as a lion. But did you ever *see* him being brave? No, I guess not. Why a hoptoad could push him around."

"You—you scalawag!" shouted Uncle Wesley furiously. "You—how dare you! Come down from there. I'll show you who's boss around here."

"O.K., old hero," said the squirrel. "I'll be right down."

"Oh, go away, you," said Alice. "We don't want you here."

"O.K., lady," said the squirrel. "You're the one that's boss. And don't forget it. —Hey, look at old Up-and-at-'em," he said, throwing a nut at Uncle Wesley, who was edging towards the brook. Then with a flirt of his tail he jumped into the next tree and vanished.

"An impossible person," said Uncle Wesley. "I find it is always best not to pay any attention to vulgar people. They—"

"Are you ready to go with us?" interrupted Alice.

Uncle Wesley looked sharply from Alice to Emma, and back again. Then he pulled himself together and gave what he hoped was a hearty laugh. "You must let your uncle have his little joke," he said. "Nothing—nothing in the world could keep me from sharing this adventure with you. I perhaps merely wanted to be quite sure that, after all these years, you really wanted your old uncle back." He hesitated, but neither of them said anything. "Well, well," he went on briskly, "what are we waiting for? No hanging back, no weak flinching from the task before us. And your old uncle, whom I'm afraid you were a bit doubtful of, will show you how an adventure should be met!"

Chapter 13

Uncle Wesley was rather quiet on the first part of the return journey, but gradually he picked up spirit, and by the time they reached the wood road he was lecturing them in quite the old style. And Alice and Emma were saying: "Yes, Uncle Wesley," and "No, Uncle Wesley," just as they had used to. But they weren't feeling the same way about Uncle Wesley as they had used to. For they knew now that he was not the hero he had pretended to be.

It was quite a blow to them. But they had been told so often, and had it so drilled into them, that they were poor weak timid creatures, that they still kept on acting that way. And so Uncle Wesley laid down the law, and they said: "Yes, Uncle Wesley," and "You are always so right, Uncle Wesley." But they weren't happy about it, as they had used to be.

By and by they got back to the balloon, and Mr. Webb came galloping down his ladder to greet Uncle Wesley, and hear about their trip, and tell them that Freddy hadn't come back yet. Uncle Wesley hadn't laid down the law quite so much during the last quarter mile, which was hard going and made him puff, but when he got his breath back, he started in again. He talked about travel. Travel, he said, was very broadening, and a valuable experience for those who, like Alice and Emma, had always lived sheltered lives. But such rough, and even dangerous travel was not the sort of thing they should attempt. And as for ballooning—well, he had no words, he said, to express his opinion of how vulgar and unladylike it was. And then he used about ten thousand words expressing it. It was quite like old times.

As they could not get back into the balloon basket, they had to wait on the ground. Mr. Webb listened for a while, and then he gave an angry snort and went back up the ladder. Uncle Wesley didn't hear the snort, of course.

Mr. Webb snorted several times more after he got back to where Mrs. Webb was sitting, and at last she said: "Well, what is it?"

"What is what?" asked Mr. Webb.

"You snorted just the way Mr. Bean does when he's reading the newspaper and wants Mrs. Bean to ask him what he's disgusted about."

"I'm disgusted about that Wesley," said Mr. Webb. "How on earth those ducks ever stood him all those years! And now they try to get him back!"

"Well, after all he's their uncle. There's such a thing as family feeling, father."

"Yes, and there's such a thing as not knowing when you're well off."

"Well," said Mrs. Webb, "I daresay you're

right. If you got all swelled up like Wesley, and started telling me everything I did was wrong, I'd just quietly drop you overboard some night when we were sailing along in the balloon." She laughed comfortably. She had a laugh a good deal like Mrs. Bean's, only, of course, smaller. "And I wouldn't go looking for you afterward," she added. "But if you ask me, Alice and Emma are going to find out before long that they had a pretty good time while their uncle was away, and from that to wishing he was gone again isn't very far. And after all—well, I don't think Uncle Wesley is going to have as much fun as he used to."

Uncle Wesley was having plenty of fun now, though. He had a lot of back lecturing to make up, and the afternoon faded into evening, and the twilight waned, and the dark came, and still his voice went on. But just as it got so dark that Alice and Emma couldn't see him any more, there came a sudden crashing of branches from the direction of the wood road. And Uncle Wesley stopped.

The crashing grew louder.

"Mercy, what can that be?" said Alice. "It

sounds like a tank going through the woods, and it's coming this way too. We must do something, sister."

"What can we do?" said Emma. "Oh, Alice, I'm so frightened! Where's Uncle Wesley? He'll protect us. Won't you, uncle?"

There was no answer.

"Uncle Wesley!" they both called.

And Uncle Wesley's voice, shaking with terror, replied faintly: "Save yourselves, my dears. Your old uncle will p-protect your retreat."

"But where are you?"

Uncle Wesley was under a log, but when they tried to seek shelter beside him, he pushed them out, protesting that there wasn't room for more than one. "Save yourselves," he repeated. "Your legs are younger than mine; you'll get away."

The crashing was very close now, and really terrifying, and then a lantern became visible, swaying high up among the trees, and behind it a white-turbaned figure, sitting cross-legged apparently upon nothing, and moving towards them ten feet up in the air.

"Oh!" exclaimed Emma weakly. "Oh! Uncle Wesley! I think I—I shall faint away!"

And sure enough, Freddy it was . . .

But Alice's sharp eyes had seen the face beneath the turban. "Wait," she said. "Don't faint yet, Emma. It's Freddy. He's come back."

And sure enough, Freddy it was, seated on Hannibal's back, as the elephant held the lantern high in his trunk. And behind came Louise, the smaller elephant.

"Ha, ha!" said Uncle Wesley, coming out from under the log. "I knew it all the time! Wanted to see if you girls would really lose your heads in such a situation. And of course you did. Tut, tut, I'm afraid you're not the stuff of which true adventurers are made."

"Oh, hush up!" said Alice sharply, and Uncle Wesley was so amazed at this sudden revolt against his authority, that he did hush up for nearly two minutes.

The elephants hung their lanterns on convenient branches, and when they had lifted Freddy and the ducks up into the balloon basket, Freddy let out enough of the grapnel rope so that the balloon was clear of the treetops. And then Hannibal and Louise took hold of the grapnel and started to tow the balloon back to South Pharisee.

Everything went smoothly, for the elephants had red lanterns tied to their tails, and though when they got on the highroad some passing motorists got a good deal of a shock, nobody bumped into them. The mice caused some trouble at first, for they were so anxious to try their parachutes that they kept jumping out and floating to the ground, and then of course they had to be picked up and put back in the basket. The elephants didn't like this much. Elephants are always a little afraid of mice. I suppose there are no animals bigger than themselves for them to be afraid of, and as they have to be afraid of something, they sort of start at the bottom again and pick out the smallest animal there is. I don't know how else to explain it.

Everybody else in the circus had gone to bed right after the last performance, but Leo had waited up for them, and when they got back to the circus grounds he helped them moor the balloon securely. Then he invited them to spend the night with him. The ducks were a little nervous about spending the night in a lion's cage, and the mice were too interested in the balloon to leave it, but Freddy accepted.

It was a long time before Freddy and Leo got to sleep. There was the gossip of the farm and the circus to exchange, and old friends to talk over, and above all, the plans for the following day.

"I've brought the balloon back," said the pig, "and Mr. Golcher can make his ascension tomorrow all right, and I won't be sent to jail. But that won't bring Mr. Bean back his money. I'll have to get it somewhere."

"Don't look at me," said the lion with a laugh. "I've never been able to save a penny in my life, never. Had plenty of it in my time, too. Doesn't stick to my paws, somehow. But whatever I have is yours, Freddy; you know that. Teeth, claws, and a good loud roar. That's all there is. But if you can use 'em . . ."

Freddy thanked his friend warmly for this generous offer. "But I don't see," he said, "what you can do. Mr. Golcher will walk off with four hundred dollars and we can't touch him." He yawned. "Well, let's sleep on it. Maybe we'll think of something."

"Have a little something before you go to bed?" asked Leo. "Cup of cocoa, or something?

No? Well, pleasant dreams." And the two animals curled up and went to sleep.

The first thing in the morning they went over to where the balloon was moored, and there was Mr. Golcher, and with him was Mr. Boomschmidt. They were watching some men pull the balloon down closer to the ground. Freddy was a little nervous, but as soon as Mr. Golcher caught sight of him, he came forward with his hand outstretched.

"Ah, the estimable Freddy. Well, no hard feelings, eh? You'll be glad to know that I have assured the police of your innocence. There'll be no further question of arresting you. We've examined the valve cord and found that it was quite impossible for you to bring the balloon down. Golcher was wrong, and Golcher apologized, and here's Golcher's hand on it. So we'll just let bygones be bygones, eh?"

"Well, I don't know," said Freddy. "Mr. Boomschmidt is going to give you two hundred dollars to make an ascension this afternoon, isn't he?"

"Right," said Mr. Golcher, rubbing his hands. "And dirt cheap, too."

"But," said Freddy, "you've already been paid two hundred by Mr. Bean, to make up for what you told him you'd lose by not making the ascension. And I think you ought to give that back."

"My gracious, so do I," said Mr. Boomschmidt. "Eh, Golcher, how about it? You can't be paid for making an ascension and for not making an ascension. Can he, Leo?"

"Not when it's the same ascension," said the lion.

"Golcher could argue that point," said Mr. Golcher, "and Golcher will. Mind you, Golcher admits nothing. But what you're saying is that I can't be paid for both making and not making the same ascension. And yet, according to you, that is what has happened. So where's your argument? You say something has happened, and then you turn around and say it can't happen. It don't make sense to Golcher."

"Dear me," said Mr. Boomschmidt, "you seem to have something there. Eh, Freddy? What do you say to that?"

"I say he's trying to mix us up," said the pig. "I told you and Leo about it, Mr. Boomschmidt, and there isn't any use arguing. Mr. Golcher got his balloon back in time for the ascension, and so he ought to give Mr. Bean's money back."

"Golcher admits nothing," repeated the balloonist. "If Mr. Bean thinks he has a claim against me, he can go to law about it. If he can prove he paid me two hundred dollars, the judge will make me pay it back. Has he got a receipt for it? Has he got any witnesses that he gave me two hundred dollars?"

"He's got me," said Freddy. "I saw him give it to you."

"You weren't there," said Mr. Golcher.

"Where?" said Mr. Boomschmidt. "You mean, where the money was paid? Well then, my goodness, you admit that Mr. Bean gave it to you!"

"Golcher admits nothing," said Mr. Golcher, looking rather embarrassed. Then he recovered himself. "Of course Freddy wasn't there," he went on. "How could he have been there, when the money wasn't paid? There wasn't any 'there' to be."

"Oh, dear," said Mr. Boomschmidt, pushing

his hat back on his head perplexedly. "Oh, dear me! I can't get this straight at all. Leo, can you—"

"I was there, behind a bush," interrupted Freddy. "And I'm a witness."

"A pig!" exclaimed Mr. Golcher.

"Pig's good enough for me," said Mr. Boomschmidt. "Freddy, here—his word's as good as his bond. My goodness, I don't know but it's better."

But Mr. Golcher shook his head. "Take it to law," he said. "Golcher's a law-abiding man. If the judge says: 'Pay it,' Golcher pays it. That's what the law's for—to tell us what's right and what's wrong. If there's an argument, Golcher says let the judge decide. That's fair, ain't it? Golcher's an honest man."

"I don't think you're honest," said Leo bluntly.

"All are entitled to their opinions, even lions," said Mr. Golcher. He spoke respectfully, and edged away from Leo, for it was his first visit to the Boomschmidt circus, and he hadn't quite got used to social intimacy with the larger carniverous animals.

"Well," said Freddy, "will you let Mr. Boomschmidt judge this case?"

"No," said Mr. Golcher. "Mr. Boomschmidt's a fine man. He knows the circus from anteater to zebra. But he don't know the law. He ain't made a study of it. And not having made a study of it, he'd be the first to acknowledge that he hasn't the special experience to handle a law case."

"I don't know that I'd acknowledge that," said Mr. Boomschmidt.

"Well, I'll acknowledge it for you," said Mr. Golcher. "No, no, my young friend," he said, patting Freddy kindly on the shoulder, "let's just drop the matter, shall we? Good grief, money ain't everything in the world! 'Tain't healthy for a young smart fellow like you to have such a greed for money. Take Golcher's advice—"

"It's not my money," said Freddy. "But I see you've made up your mind to keep it, so I won't argue any more." He thought a minute. "Well," he said, "I've got to get the money somewhere, because it was my fault that Mr. Bean had to pay it out. So maybe . . ." He looked thoughtfully at Mr. Golcher. "Over at Centerboro, on the Fourth, you said that it was hard to get a crowd for a balloon ascension unless you had some specially exciting features. You thought it would be something new if I made a speech, and then went up. Well, my jaws got stuck on some candy, and I couldn't speak when the time came. But you did get a big crowd all the same. Now suppose I really made a speech this time, and then went up with you. And suppose we took along four mice who would make a parachute jump when the balloon got up a ways. If you'd pay me something for that, then I'd have at least a start in paying Mr. Bean back."

But Mr. Golcher shook his head. "I get two hundred for the ascension anyway," he said. "Talking pigs and jumping mice is nice—Golcher don't deny it. But I won't get any more money by adding them to the show. 'Tain't business to give more than you're paid for. Anyway, you owe me a speech for the one you didn't make last time."

"All right," said Freddy. "I'll go up with you and make a speech for nothing. I wouldn't want to be in debt to you for even a speech. But how about the mice? Would you pay ten dollars to have them do their jump?"

"Golcher wouldn't pay a penny," said the balloonist emphatically. "If Mr. Boomschmidt wants to pay for 'em, if he wants some extra frills on the ascension, why that's up to him."

"How about it, Mr. Boomschmidt?" asked Freddy.

Mr. Boomschmidt's fancy had been tickled by a phrase that Mr. Golcher had used. "Mice is nice," he chuckled. "Did you hear that, Leo? That's good, that is! Mice is nice. And how about lions? Lions is what, Leo? Give me a word."

"Lions is—well, lions is—" Leo frowned thoughtfully.

"Ha!" said Mr. Boomschmidt triumphantly. "We've stumped Leo. Eh, Leo? Admit you're stumped."

Leo grinned. "Leo admits nothing," he said. "Because Leo says the whole thing's wrong, chief. You can't say: Lions *is*. It's: Lions *are*."

"Why, that's right," said Mr. Boomschmidt. "Of course, Leo. See here, Golcher; you can't say: Mice *is*. It's not grammar. It's—"

"Listen, boss," said Leo, twitching Mr. Boomschmidt's sleeve. "Freddy's making you a proposition."

"Mice *is*," murmured Mr. Boomschmidt. "Eh? Oh yes, Freddy. Shoot."

So Freddy asked him again, and Mr. Boomschmidt was delighted with the idea. He would pay five dollars per mouse, he said.

"Four mice at five dollars is twenty dollars," said Leo. "That's twice what Freddy offered them to Golcher for, boss."

"Now don't try to beat me down, Leo," said Mr. Boomschmidt.

"I'm not. I'm trying to show you that you've beat yourself up. But it's all right; you can afford it. And how about ducks? Freddy's got some duck jumpers, too."

"Ducks?" said Mr. Boomschmidt. "Not as sensational as mice. Sort of—well, *you* know: fluff. Let's say two-fifty per— Hey, wait! How many ducks?"

"Three," said Freddy. "But I'm not too sure of Uncle Wesley."

"Two-fifty per duck, then," said Mr. Boomschmidt. "Or is that too much, Leo? My gracious, you can buy a duck outright for a dollar or so."

"But you can't make him jump for a dollar," said the lion.

"How do you know—have you ever tried, Leo? Oh well, never mind. Is it settled, then? I'll pay you after the show, Freddy. Come on, Leo; we've got to have a talk with Willy." He turned to Mr. Golcher. "He's our thirty-foot boa constrictor. And you know what he did last night? He was invited to supper at Cephas Pratt's, but he got mixed up and went to Zenas Pratt's, and of course they didn't expect him, and when he came looping in the kitchen door, they went out the kitchen window. Willy thought it was funny, and I suppose in a way it was, but he hadn't ought to have done what he did because he ought to have seen they weren't expecting him. Their supper was on the table and he ate it all—a ham and a roast chicken and a lot of vegetables and jelly and pickles and a big chocolate cake. Come on, Leo. Willy will have to go over to Pratts' and apologize."

Chapter 14

Although there hadn't been time to print handbills, or to get the names of Freddy and the mouse parachutists up on the posters, Mr. Boomschmidt had instructed Oscar to announce the facts about the balloon ascension to everyone buying a ticket, so that at two o'clock, the time announced, a large crowd had assembled. Men stood at the ropes, ready to cast the balloon off, the mice and ducks were lined up on the edge of the basket, and when Freddy and

Mr. Golcher climbed up the little stepladder and got in, a loud cheer went up.

"Well now, make your speech," said Mr. Golcher, "and we'll push off." He glanced up at the big bag of the balloon which hung above them. "She seems a little heavy. Maybe we ought to have got more gas in her. But I guess we'll go up all right." He stumbled, and looked down at his feet. "What's all this stuff in here?"

"There does seem to be a lot more of it," said Freddy. "I guess maybe we didn't pack the blankets and boxes very well."

"Well, we can fix it after we start," said Mr. Golcher. "We can't have all these piles of stuff underfoot. But get on with your speech."

So Freddy leaned over the edge of the basket. "Ladies and gentlemen," he said. "Friends and well wishers, animal and human; citizens of South Pharisee, Clamville, Upper Cattawampus, Bounding Brook, and all communities thereto appertaining and with them connected in whatsoever fashion and by whatsoever means, I greet you." And then he stopped.

"Get on with it; get on with it," said Mr. Golcher impatiently.

But Freddy realized suddenly that he didn't know what to say. He had been so busy wondering how he was to get the two hundred back that he had forgotten that he had a speech to make, and now here he was with a large audience hanging breathless upon his words, and there weren't any words for them to hang on.

But he had to say something. "Un—unaccustomed as I am," he went on nervously, "to appearing before such a large and distinguished audience as I now see before me, I feel that no words of mine can express the great honor which you have done me. It is indeed a pleasure and a privilege to address you, and I wish to say that—that—"

He stopped again, but only for a moment. For suddenly he knew what he would say. "At Centerboro on the Fourth," he said, "I went up in this same balloon. The valve cord was stuck, and I couldn't get down. But Mr. Golcher thought I had stolen it, and had the police looking for me. He also went to my owner, Mr. Bean, and demanded and obtained from him two hundred dollars. That two hundred was to pay him for—"

"Here! None of that!" said Mr. Golcher angrily, and he seized Freddy by the shoulder and pulled him back, at the same time giving a signal to the men to cast off.

"Go on!" shouted the crowd. "Let him talk!"

The balloon, released from its moorings, gave a lurch and started off, but instead of going up into the air, it swept across the circus grounds with the basket barely clearing the heads of the crowd, who ducked and ran in all directions.

Hastily, Mr. Golcher threw out half a dozen bags of sand that were hung on the sides of the basket, and the balloon rose a little, but sluggishly, and barely enough to keep them from catching on the tall fence that separated the circus grounds from the open fields.

"Feels as if she was full of lead," said Mr. Golcher perplexedly. "Can't understand it. There should be enough gas in the bag to lift our weight." He threw out the last of the sand and they gained a few feet more. "Not enough," he said. "We'll foul those trees when we get across the valley. Well, pig, I guess one of us has got to jump out." He grinned angrily at Freddy. "And that one ain't Golcher."

"It isn't Freddy, either," said the pig firmly.

"If your old balloon won't go up, pull the valve cord and bring it down."

"When Golcher gets paid for an ascension, he makes an ascension," replied the balloonist. "Bring her down, hey? You don't suppose Boomschmidt will pay two hundred for this performance, do you?"

Freddy looked over the side. They were traveling with the breeze at a pretty good rate of speed, and the ground was ten feet below the edge of the basket. It looked pretty hard, and there were stones in it. Still . . .

"Give me Mr. Bean's two hundred dollars and I'll jump," said Freddy bravely.

Alice and Emma began quacking excitedly. "No, no, Freddy. Good gracious, you'll be broken to pieces."

"It won't hurt him in the slightest," said Uncle Wesley. "Do be quiet, my dears."

"Well, I'm going to jump out," said Alice. "That will lighten the balloon some. Come, Emma."

"Yes, sister," said Emma obediently. And they jumped and fluttered to the ground.

The balloon went up perhaps a foot.

"We can jump too," said Eeek, adjusting his parachute. "What do you say, boys?"

"Sure," said Cousin Augustus. "But how about Wesley? Scared, duck?"

"Don't be ridiculous," said Uncle Wesley in a superior tone. "If you can show me one good reason why I should make a public exhibition of myself in this vulgar way—"

"*One* good reason!" exclaimed Eeny. He winked at the other mice. "Here's four good reasons. Come on, boys." And they rushed at the duck, nipping at him with their sharp little teeth, and pushed him struggling and protesting to the edge.

"Stop!" he quacked. "This is an outrage! This is—ouch! Oh! You're killing me—you're—oh!" And with a despairing quack he fell.

A distant cheer from the spectators they had left behind, came to the balloonists. For the sight of four mice, floating to earth on tiny parachutes, was, even at that distance, a remarkable sight. But even with Uncle Wesley and the mice gone, the balloon plainly would not clear the trees towards which they were rapidly drifting.

"You're next, pig," said Mr. Golcher.

"Give me Mr. Bean's money and I'll jump," said Freddy.

Mr. Golcher started to reach for him, and then drew back. It wouldn't be easy to throw Freddy out, because a pig is almost as hard to get hold of as a seal, and everybody knows that that is practically impossible. Mr. Golcher glanced at the approaching trees, then he said: "Ha! Golcher's a fair man. Golcher'll make you a sporting proposition. He'll wrestle you for it. If you can put Golcher down, he'll pay you the two hundred and you can jump. But if Golcher puts you down, you'll jump without the money."

"I don't think that's very fair," said Freddy, "but I want that money, so I'll do it."

"No fair biting," said Mr. Golcher, and grabbed Freddy around the neck.

Freddy's legs were too short to be of any use in a wrestling match, and he couldn't do much to put Mr. Golcher down. About all he could do was to struggle out of the different holds that Mr. Golcher got on him, and keep from being put down himself. They thrashed and rolled and kicked, and Freddy began to pick up hope, for every time he felt himself being forced down on his back, something strange seemed to happen to Mr. Golcher. He seemed to slip or trip over the huge pile of blankets that took up so much of the basket, and Freddy was able to pull free. And then suddenly Mr. Golcher seemed to have a convulsion, and he fell on his back and lay there with Freddy on top of him.

"I win," panted Freddy, and got up. But Mr. Golcher lay still.

"Oh, goodness," said Freddy, "I hope I haven't killed him!" And then he looked more closely and saw that an enormous paw was resting on Mr. Golcher's chest. And the paw was attached to a huge forearm covered with tawny fur, that came out from under the blankets. "Leo!" he exclaimed.

The blankets heaved, and the lion's head came out. "Congratulations, old boy," it said. "That was a great fight you put up." He took his paw off Mr. Golcher's chest. "Get up, mister," he said, "and give this boy his money." And as Mr. Golcher slowly opened his eyes, the lion bared his teeth and gave a rumbling growl that made the basket vibrate.

There was a gurgling noise in Mr. Golcher's throat, and his eyes kept on opening until they were twice as wide open as usual, and his mouth came open at the same time, and all at once a big yell came out of it, and he leaped up and vaulted right over the edge of the basket. And as the balloon, relieved of his weight, shot up into the air, they looked down and saw him slipping and slithering to earth through the branches of a small tree which had fortunately broken his fall.

"Oh, Leo! He's hurt," exclaimed Freddy.

"That's cherry juice on his face, not blood," said Leo. "That's a cherry tree."

"Yes, and that bulge in his back pocket is Mr. Bean's two hundred dollars," said Freddy. "Not that I couldn't have taken it, anyway, for I didn't lick him, and I didn't jump. Leo, you oughtn't to have interfered."

"Well, dye my hair!" said the lion. "Is that the thanks I get for spending two hours under a pile of hot blankets on a day when it's ninety in the shade? You carry your honesty too far, pal. That money doesn't belong to Golcher, and

"Leo!" he exclaimed.

any way we can get it back to its rightful owner is an honest way."

"Maybe you're right. And I've got an idea, Leo. See what you think of it. —Hey, what's the matter?" For Leo had leaned his head against the side of the basket and closed his eyes.

"Feel queer," muttered the lion, waving a feeble paw. "Awful queer. Might have been— baked beans I had for supper last night. Ugh, mustn't think of that. Let me down out of here."

"Maybe you're a little seasick." Freddy saw that they had passed over the trees and were drifting across a wide hay field. He pulled the valve cord, and in a moment they began slowly to go down. A few minutes later they stepped out of the basket, and having let most of the gas out of the balloon, so that the half-collapsed bag rested like a giant mushroom on the ground, they started back towards the circus.

But they had taken only a few steps when Freddy turned around. "I forgot the Webbs," he said. So he went back and got the spiders, but when he rejoined Leo, the lion was stretched out flat on the ground.

"Leave me, my friend," moaned Leo tragically. "There is nothing you can do for me now. Tell Mr. Boomschmidt: just a small tomb—nothing expensive or ostentatious. With a few words carved on it. Perhaps you would write a suitable epitaph, Freddy. Just some modest and unassuming sentiment—"

"Nonsense," said Freddy briskly. "You aren't going to die, Leo."

"You think not?" murmured Leo. "You take from me my last hope."

Freddy looked at him and grinned. "H'm," he said thoughtfully; "perhaps I am wrong. You look pretty bad. Of course, dying from seasickness—well, it's sort of ridiculous, sort of like being run down by a baby carriage. But don't worry. I won't let anybody laugh, or say slighting things. I'll stand up for—"

"Funny, eh?" Leo jumped to his feet. "Just let 'em try laughing, that's all!" He glared ferociously.

"Come on," said Freddy. "I want to try my plan."

Chapter 15

Although the balloon ascension had been rather
a fizzle, it had entertained the crowd, Mr. Boomschmidt said, and so he paid Mr. Golcher the
two hundred dollars agreed on. When Leo and
Freddy got back to the circus, Mr. Golcher arranged at once to have a truck go out and bring
in the balloon. "And then," he said, "Golcher
is leaving this part of the country for good. And
the next time Golcher gets chummy with a pig,
the pig'll be on a platter, and Golcher'll have

his napkin tucked under his chin."

Freddy thought this remark in rather bad taste, but he only said: "Well, we might finish our wrestling match first, Mr. Golcher."

"Oh," said Mr. Golcher; "so you admit you didn't win, eh?"

"Of course I didn't. I didn't know Leo was there. My goodness, I didn't need Leo. I could win without his help."

"You and a couple of hippopotamuses, maybe," said Mr. Golcher.

"You and me in a ring together, and no lions or any other animals anywhere around, and Mr. Boomschmidt as referee. How about it?"

"My gracious," put in Mr. Boomschmidt, "what a show that would be! Eh, Leo? Wrestling match between a man and a pig; best two out of three falls and no holds barred. Oh, *oh,* how that would pack 'em in!"

Mr. Golcher became interested. "You'd pay for that, Boomschmidt?"

Mr. Boomschmidt said he'd pay a hundred dollars.

"All of it to go to the winner," said Mr. Golcher quickly.

"That's all right with me," said Freddy. "But what I'm wrestling you for, Mr. Golcher, is Mr. Bean's two hundred dollars. If I win, you hand it over."

"Yeah," said Mr. Golcher, "and if *I* win, what do *you* hand over?"

"Why should he hand over anything, for goodness' sake?" demanded Mr. Boomschmidt. "That two hundred—"

"Wait a minute, chief," put in Leo. "No use arguing with a crook. If—"

"Who's a crook?" demanded Mr. Golcher.

"You are," said Leo, "and what are you going to do about it?" And he held up one forepaw and examined his three-inch claws thoughtfully.

"I—er . . . well, I'm not going to do anything, I guess," said Mr. Golcher lamely.

"O.K. Then, as I say: no use arguing with a crook. As I see it, Freddy will have to put up something, or Golcher won't play. What do you say, Freddy?"

"I haven't got anything to put up."

"Then we'll just wrestle for the hundred dollars," said Mr. Golcher.

But Freddy said no, they'd wrestle on his terms or not at all.

Mr. Golcher argued, but in the end he agreed. He was sure he could win, and that meant another hundred dollars in his pocket. He didn't think there was the slightest chance of his having to give up Mr. Bean's money.

So it was arranged that the match should be put on right after the big show, which was about to begin. Freddy went into Leo's cage to rest up, and while Mr. Boomschmidt went in to take part in the show, Leo made the necessary arrangements. There was a large bandstand near the big tent, roofed over, but open at the sides except for a wooden railing. Leo had the railing taken down and ropes put up, and the floor covered with canvas. And then the enclosure around the bandstand was roped off, so that admission fees could be collected from the spectators. And then he made a few other arrangements.

When the big show was over, Leo woke Freddy and brought him over to the bandstand. Several hundred crowded around the stand, and as the lion and the pig worked their way through, many of them pushed forward to whack Freddy on the back and shout encouragement, for nearly everybody now knew about the two hundred dollars and hoped that he would get it back. Mr. Boomschmidt, as referee, was already on the platform, introducing Mr. Golcher. "In this corner, ladies and gentlemen, Henry P. Golcher, known as the Bounding Balloonist."

Mr. Golcher, dressed in a blue silk robe with a large G on the breast pocket, rose and shook his clenched fists above his head.

"And in this corner," went on Mr. Boomschmidt, as Freddy climbed through the ropes, "that well known figure, that paragon of pugnacity, Freddy, the Perilous Pig!" He paused for the applause. "And now, ladies and gentlemen, this match will be for a purse of one hundred dollars, generously donated by Boomschmidt's Colossal and Unparalleled Circus. The best two out of three falls; no biting, gouging, scratching, no chawing or gnawing; and may the best man—or my goodness, the best pig! —win! Go!"

Mr. Golcher rose, tossed off the robe, and

stood revealed in the close-fitting blue tights and star-spangled trunks he sometimes wore in his balloon ascensions. There were some cheers, for he was a fine figure of a man, though a little thin. He smiled confidently as he moved in a crouching position towards the center of the ring. Freddy tried to smile confidently, too, but he wasn't very successful. Still, he felt that he had a chance of winning. He had no hands, of course, with which to grab Mr. Golcher, and his legs were too short to get any sort of a hold with. But like every pig, he was a past master at wriggling. He was pretty sure that he could wriggle out of any hold Mr. Golcher got on him. And then, too, to get a decision, Mr. Golcher would have to put him down on his back—and a pig's back is a good deal rounder than a man's. As Freddy sized up the situation, it would be almost impossible for him to put Mr. Golcher on his back. But if he could wriggle and stall until Mr. Golcher got thoroughly tired out and winded, then he would have a chance.

And since the thing to do was to get Mr. Golcher winded, Freddy charged out of his corner at the run and drove straight at Mr. Golcher's stomach. The balloonist hadn't expected this, and he tried to sidestep. But it was too late. They came together with a smack, and Mr. Golcher said "Wha-a-a-a-a!" and sat down.

Freddy was pretty pleased with himself and would have liked to stop and acknowledge the cheers, but he knew he must follow up his advantage. Mr. Golcher had rolled over and was lying flat on his stomach, trying to gain time until he got his wind back. He was too close to the ground for Freddy to butt him again, so the pig jumped up in the air and came down heavily on Mr. Golcher's back. Mr. Golcher said "Wha-a-a-a!" again, only not so loud this time, and lay without moving. And as he lay there, helpless, Freddy managed to roll him over on his back.

"First fall for Freddy!" shouted Mr. Boomschmidt. The crowd cheered itself hoarse, and Hannibal, who had been appointed to act as second for Mr. Golcher, reached out with his trunk and dragged his principal back into his corner, where he propped him up in the chair and fanned him with his big ears.

Back in his own corner, Freddy relaxed and listened to the advice which his second, Leo,

But it was too late.

was whispering in his ear. "You're doing fine. But look out for him; he's plenty tough. Look at him: he's pretending to feel a lot worse than he does. Be careful."

"I will," said Freddy. But he had no intention of being careful. Mr. Golcher looked pretty done up to him. And when Mr. Boomschmidt said: "Go!" and Mr. Golcher staggered out of his chair, he rushed out of his corner just as he had before.

But Mr. Golcher was ready this time. With a swift turn he twisted aside, and Freddy missed him entirely and charged right across the platform and through the ropes and came down Plump! on a little boy named Jimmy Wiggs, who was one of his warmest admirers. This was lucky for Freddy, because although it knocked the wind out of him, he wasn't really hurt. But it wasn't so lucky for the little boy, who had to be taken home and put to bed with a hot water bottle. It shows how much he admired Freddy, though, that as they carried him off, he said: "I hope Freddy wins."

The spectators hoisted Freddy back on to the platform, and some of them wanted the match to stop until he got his wind back, but even Freddy admitted that this wouldn't be fair. And so Mr. Golcher won that fall with ease.

"I told you to be careful," said Leo. "Now this time, lay off that butting. Close in and wrestle. After all, this isn't a collision contest."

When Mr. Boomschmidt said: "Go!" for the third time, the two contestants approached each other warily, Freddy on all fours, Mr. Golcher crouching, with one arm guarding his stomach. Then suddenly Mr. Golcher darted forward and caught Freddy by the leg, and in two seconds they were at it hammer and tongs, rolling and thumping about the platform. Hold after hold Mr. Golcher tried, and each time Freddy managed to wriggle free. But no sooner had he escaped from one hold than another was clamped on him, and each time his shoulders got closer to the canvas. He could see Mr. Boomschmidt dancing about them, peering at his shoulders, watching for them both to touch the floor at the same time. He caught a glimpse of Leo, shaking his head hopelessly. He wriggled for all he was worth, but relentlessly he was forced down. His left shoulder-blade was on the canvas, his right one went down, down—and then suddenly something happened to Mr. Golcher. He gave a sort of yelp and slapped at the back of his neck. And Freddy, partly released, slipped away.

Mr. Golcher had him again in a second though, and the struggle went on. And then the same thing happened all over again. With Mr. Golcher's left arm around his neck, and Mr. Golcher's right arm locked about his left hind leg, he was panting and wriggling desperately to keep from being pressed flat, when an electric shock seemed to go through his opponent, who again yelped and, letting go with his left arm, clawed at his neck.

Time after time the same thing happened. Freddy hardly had to struggle at all. He just waited until he was almost down, and at the last moment each time something happened to Mr. Golcher so that Freddy could wriggle free. It was a good deal like the struggle in the balloon basket, when Leo had been secretly helping, but there was certainly nobody on the platform but themselves and Mr. Boomschmidt, whose anxious face kept appearing to Freddy, now upside down, now sidewise, now right side up, as bent over the wrestlers.

One thing was certain, though. Mr. Golcher was getting tired. He had all but had the decision a dozen times, and the effort was beginning to tell on him. He was panting heavily, and his grip was becoming weaker, his movements slower. To the spectators, it began to look like a slow motion picture of a wrestling match. And then all at once he gave a moan and fell limply across the pig. Freddy wriggled out, then getting his snout under Mr. Golcher, rolled him over on his back.

"Third fall for Freddy!" shouted Mr. Boomschmidt. He seized Freddy's right fore trotter and help it up. "Ladies and gentlemen, the winner! Freddy, the Perilous Pig, wins the hundred dollar purse so generously donated by Boomschmidt's Colossal and Unparalleled Circus." He handed the roll of bills to the pig.

The cheers rocked the bandstand, as Mr. Golcher got slowly to his knees. He was trying to say something, but the noise was so great that nobody could hear him until Mr. Boomschmidt held up his hand for silence.

"And now," said Mr. Boomschmidt, "a word from Mr. Henry P. Golcher, the Bounding Balloonist, whose gallant effort, though doomed to defeat, will be remembered as long as the beautiful village of South Pharisee continues to stand, mirrored in the calm waters of Bounding Brook. A gallant fight, my friends, which deserves to go down in history with Thermopylae, with the Alamo, with Boomschmidt's—"

"Hey, boss," interrupted Leo; "let him talk."

"Eh?" said Mr. Boomschmidt. "My goodness, of course. Now, Mr. Golcher?"

"He wouldn't have won," panted Mr. Golcher, "if somebody hadn't kept sticking pins in me."

"Pins?" said Mr. Boomschmidt.

"Look at the back of my neck," said Mr. Golcher, turning around.

"No pins there," said Mr. Boomschmidt.

"Of course there aren't. But you can see where they were stuck into me."

"Little red spots," said Mr. Boomschmidt. "H'm, yes. Maybe you're coming down with the measles, Golcher. My goodness, Leo, how awful that would be! None of our animals have ever had measles, have they? Golcher, you must leave. Measles are catching."

" 'Is,' boss," said Leo.

"Is, boss?" repeated Mr. Boomschmidt, frowning at the lion. "What kind of talk is that, Leo? Really, you get harder to understand every day. What on earth—"

"Measles *is*," said Leo. "Measles is singular."

"Won't be singular if all the elephants and tigers and hyenas get them. Mice is; measles is," he muttered. "I can never get these things straight. But, see here, Golcher—"

"Wait a minute," said Freddy. "In the darkness up under the roof of the bandstand his eye had caught a tiny gleam of light—such a glimmer as a strand of cobweb will make when it catches the sunlight. And looking more closely, he saw that there was indeed a long strand hanging down from the center of the roof, and ending just over his head. And right at the end was Mr. Webb, looking—Freddy thought, though it is always hard, even close up, to tell about a spider's expression—very pleased with himself.

"Mr. Golcher is right," he said. "It wasn't pins, though; it was a friend of mine, a spider.

He slid down and bit you on the neck, every time you were about to win. I'm sorry. I suppose he thought he was helping me. But it wasn't fair. This money doesn't belong to me." And he handed the hundred dollars to Mr. Golcher. "You'd have won," he said. "I guess this belongs to you."

Mr. Golcher looked at the pig in amazement. "You mean you—you're *giving* it to me?"

"I lost," said Freddy. "At least, I would have if the match had been fair."

Mr. Golcher frowned and fingered the bills uneasily. "Yeah," he said. "Guess that's so. You could have kept it—I suppose you know that? Nobody knew about the spider. Referee didn't see him, and what the referee don't see, don't count. Yeah." He looked up quickly at Freddy, then down at the money in his hand. "Do you *like* being honest?" he asked.

"Not exactly," said Freddy truthfully.

"Then why do you do it when you don't have to?"

"I don't know. I suppose maybe because Mr. Bean thinks I'm honest. I sort of want him to be right."

"H'm," said Mr. Golcher. "Nobody ever thought *I* was honest, I guess."

"Why should they?" asked Leo drily.

Mr. Golcher didn't answer him. "I suppose I might try it some time," he said thoughtfully.

"You could try it now," said Freddy. "With that two hundred dollars."

"Now?" exclaimed Mr. Golcher. "Well, not *now*; not *today*. Golcher don't feel the strength for it today. Some day you hunt up Golcher when he's feeling good and strong, and then you try him with something small—say about ten cents, to begin with. Work him up gradual." He slipped into the robe which Hannibal held for him.

Mr. Boomschmidt had stepped to the edge of the platform and was telling the crowd what had happened. There was some grumbling among them when they learned that Mr. Golcher had taken the purse, but Mr. Boomschmidt knew how to handle an audience, and he got them into a good temper by explaining that although the rules of fair play made it necessary for Mr. Golcher to take the money, neither of the contestants had won, since it was really Mr.

Webb who had thrown Mr. Golcher the second time.

"The spider ought to get the money, then," shouted one man.

"Good gracious, what would a spider do with a hundred dollars?" said Mr. Boomschmidt.

"He could buy a lot of flies with it," said the man, and the crowd laughed and began to break up.

"Well, come on, pig," said Leo, with a glance at Mr. Golcher, who had drawn a large wallet from the pocket of his gown and was stuffing the money into it. The balloonist looked angry and uncomfortable.

"What's the matter, Golcher?" asked Leo with a grin. "Did your right hand gyp your left hand out of part of the cash?"

"Oh, mind your business," said Mr. Golcher sullenly.

"Hey, what are you so cross about?" retorted the lion. "You won the bout and collected the money. You ought to be pleased."

"I'm cross at him, if you must know," said Mr. Golcher, pointing at Freddy.

"Well, for goodness' sake!" said Freddy with

some irritation, "I don't know what call you've got to be cross at me. I gave up the money because—"

"That's just it!" interrupted Mr. Golcher. "I won the bout, didn't I? But everybody is praising you for losing it."

"Rats!" said Leo disgustedly. "They're praising him because he played fair, even though you hadn't played fair with him."

Mr. Golcher put his hands on his knees and bent down and scowled angrily into Freddy's face. "You think you're better than I am," he said furiously. "They all think you're better than I am. And Golcher can't *stand* it!" he shouted suddenly. He jumped up and, fumbling in his wallet, drew out a packet of bills and slammed them down at Freddy's feet. "Golcher ain't going to have *anybody* saying a pig is better than him!"

Freddy picked up the bills. "Two hundred," he said. "This is Mr. Bean's money. Why, Mr. Golcher—"

"Take it," interrupted Mr. Golcher, "and get out before I change my mind. Because I'm going to change it. I can feel it changing now.

It's saying to me: 'Golcher, you're being a fool. Do you want to give two hundred dollars just so folks will say you're as good as a pig?' I ain't got the strength to stand up against that kind of an argument. Go *on*! What are you waiting for?"

"Well, dye my hair!" said Leo. "If the guy wants to be honest, far be it from us to stop him. Grab your money, pig, and run."

Chapter 16

That evening after the show, Mr. Boomschmidt gave a large party for the Bean animals, and the next morning he drove them home himself in his own private car. This car was a large sedan, and was the only vehicle connected with the circus which was not painted red and gold, and decorated with pictures and signs. "Sometimes," Mr. Boomschmidt said, "I like to get away from the circus for a while, but, my goodness, if I had signs all over this car, everybody'd think I was a parade and I wouldn't get any peace and quiet. This way, I can drive around the country, and nobody knows who I am."

Freddy thought that Mr. Boomschmidt, with his silk hat and bright plaid suit, would be known anywhere, even if on the center of each door panel of the car there hadn't been the name: Boomschmidt, in red Gothic lettering, and tastefully surmounted with a small gilt crown. But of course he didn't say so.

Mr. Boomschmidt took them for a short drive before starting for the farm, and as they were passing through the village of South Pharisee, Freddy saw a little boy sitting disconsolately on the front steps of a house. He was Jimmy Wiggs, the boy that Freddy had fallen on at the wrestling match. So Mr. Boomschmidt stopped the car and Freddy got out.

The boy jumped up. "You're Freddy. Did you win the bout?"

"No," said Freddy. "Mr. Golcher won. I'm sorry I fell on you. Are you all right again?"

"Oh, sure. It didn't really hurt me. I guess it was kind of an honor, Mr. Freddy, to be fallen on by you."

"Well, I know some people that wouldn't feel that way about it," said the pig. "But who's that?" he asked, as the heads of several larger boys appeared over the hedge that separated the lawn from the yard next door, and began sticking out their tongues at Freddy, and grunting, and calling: "Oink, oink!" in disgusting voices.

"Oh, that's Jack, my older brother, and his gang. They haven't got any manners. I guess— well maybe you better go, Mr. Freddy."

Mr. Boomschmidt had got out of the car and he went towards the intruders. "My gracious, what's the matter, you boys?" he asked. "Are you sick or something? Shall I call a doctor?"

"Nah," said Jack. And he went on calling: "Oink, oink! Jimmy's talking to a pig. Is that part of your big circus, Jimmy?"

"What's this about a circus?" asked Freddy.

Jimmy explained that he and his friends, having seen the Boomschmidt show yesterday, had decided to have a circus of their own in the back yard. They had rounded up some neighborhood dogs and cats, and a chicken or two, and had put signs on them: "Most ferocious lion in captivity," and so on. They had been having a lot of fun getting the show ready, but then Jack and his gang had found out about it, and had begun to make fun of them. And that wasn't the worst of it. Jack had organized what he called the "Lion Hunters' Club," and he said that when the circus opened, he was going to unfasten the cages and let all the animals out, and then the lion hunters were going to have a big lion hunt all over the neighborhood.

"I don't care so much about his breaking up our circus," said Jimmy, "but Jack isn't very good to animals, and I'm afraid maybe Pete— he's my dog—and Mary Hughes' kitten, and some of the other pets will get hurt."

Freddy looked at Mr. Boomschmidt, and Mr. Boomschmidt looked at Freddy, and then Freddy said: "Let's see your circus grounds."

So Jimmy took them around into the back yard. There were a couple of old chicken coops, and a shed, and half a dozen crates. A dog was tied in each of the chicken coops, and two of the crates had kittens in them. Jimmy explained that the rest of the animals hadn't arrived yet. There were three of Jimmy's friends sitting in the shed doorway.

"H'm," said Freddy. "Well, Jimmy, I don't know just what we can do to help make your circus a success, but we'll come see it anyway. What time does the show start?"

Jimmy said two o'clock.

"Well, you go right ahead with your plans," said Freddy. "We'll be back."

Jimmy cheered up at this and began to thank Freddy, and Mr. Boomschmidt walked over to the fence, above which the heads of Jack and his gang were visible, shouting: "Oink, oink!" derisively.

"My goodness, boys," said Mr. Boomschmidt, "you've got it all wrong. Pigs don't say 'oink.'"

"Do too. Oink, oink!" yelled Jack.

"Dear me, I think you are the funniest people I ever saw," said Mr. Boomschmidt. "Have you heard this pig here say 'oink'? Of course you haven't. The only persons who have said 'oink' around here are you and your friends. So if you are right in believing that pigs say 'oink', then you must be pigs."

"Aw, you're just trying to mix us up," said Jack.

"Of course I am. But you'll admit I don't have to try very hard." Suddenly he drew a dollar out of his pocket. "Do you like candy?"

They stared at him with their mouths open.

"Now, look," said Mr. Boomschmidt. "If you'll promise to let Jimmy and his friends alone until they are ready to open their show, I'll give you this dollar. Is it a deal?"

"Sure, sure," said the boys, and began climbing over the fence. "But we're going to have our lion hunt just the same," said Jack.

"Oh, I don't care about your lion hunt," said Mr. Boomschmidt. "Only I hope you'll be careful not to hurt any of the animals. Remember, they can't protect themselves—"

"Oh, sure, we won't hurt 'em; we'll just chase 'em a little," said Jack, and Mr. Boomschmidt nodded and handed over the dollar.

The boys ran off, oinking merrily, and Mr. Boomschmidt turned to Jimmy. "We have to go now, but we'll be back at two. And don't worry about your pets. We'll see they don't get hurt."

At two o'clock when the Jimmy Wiggs Circus, Greatest Show on Earth, opened its doors,

Mr. Boomschmidt and Freddy were among the first to pay the admission of six bottle caps and enter the grounds. The attendance was fairly large for that kind of a show, for at least ten other persons, most of them under twelve years of age, also crowded into the back yard. And Jimmy, as proprietor, guided them from cage to cage, explaining the habits and enlarging on the ferocity of their various occupants.

"We have here," he said, stopping before the crate in which Pete, his fox terrier, was confined, "a genuine African Wampus, the only one in captivity. He has a head like an alligator and claws and a mane like a lion, and he lives exclusively on uncles and aunts. If any of you children have an uncle or aunt present, you'll have to be pretty careful, for when he sees one, he gobbles 'em up, shoes and all.

"Now in this cage," he continued, passing on to the first chicken coop, "we have—"

"Let's go on to the next cage," interrupted Freddy, pointing to a crate containing a kitten.

Jimmy had had his hand on the door of the chicken coop, which was closed, and he looked a little puzzled for a minute. Then he said: "All right," and was about to go over to the kitten, when there was a scrabbling on the other side of the fence and a shout: "Here come the lion hunters!" And Jack and three of his gang climbed over into the back yard. One of them had a BB gun.

Jimmy confronted them. "I wish you'd go away, Jack. Can't you let us—"

But Jack pushed him contemptuously aside. "So this is your old menagerie, is it? This is a hot show, this is! Well, where's your lions?" He walked over to Pete's crate. Pete was lying down, pretending to be asleep. Evidently he had some previous acquaintance with Jack.

"Here's a lion, boys," Jack shouted. "Get your guns ready, when I turn him loose—"

Mr. Boomschmidt touched Jack on the arm. "There's a bigger lion in the chicken coop," he said. "If you want a good lion skin to hang on the walls of your hunting lodge, he's your animal."

Jack looked at him suspiciously. Then he turned to Jimmy. "What you got in here?"

"Aw, Jack," pleaded Jimmy, "that's Mary's kitten in there. Please don't hunt her."

"... a genuine African Wampus, the only one in captivity."

"A lion, my men!" shouted Jack, pushing Jimmy back. "Ready?" He flung open the door of the chicken coop. And with a roar, Leo bounded out into the middle of the back yard.

With loud yelps of fear the lion hunters made for the fence. They reached the top in one bound—and stayed there. For two enormous grey shapes rose on the other side, and the long trunks of the elephants waved above their heads. Jack began to whimper.

Mr. Boomschmidt turned to the spectators, who had crowded back against the house. "Don't be frightened," he said. "We just want to give these boys a lesson in how to treat animals. You're all perfectly safe.

"Now my brave lion hunters," he said, "get down and get in that chicken coop. Get *down!*" he said sharply. "Or shall I have Leo, here, help you?"

So they got slowly down. They had to pass Leo to get into the coop, and the lion glared at each of them, licking his chops in an anticipatory way that made them tremble. And when Jack slunk past, Leo crouched and lashed his tail.

"Come, come, Leo," murmured Mr. Boom-schmidt, "don't overdo it. We want to scare 'em, but we don't want to scare 'em to death!"

When they were in the coop Mr. Boom-schmidt gave a whistle, and through the gate came a procession of animals. Nearly every animal from the circus was there—tigers, elephants, a rhino named Jerry, three hyenas, two leopards, six alligators, and last, the boa constrictor. They filed past the chicken coop, and as each animal came opposite the doorway he put his head in and stared hard at the lion hunters. None of the animals growled or snapped: they just stared hard.

Then when they had all had a good look, they lined up on one side of the yard, and Mr. Boom-schmidt ordered the boys out. "Your part of the show is over," he said. "And you can go if you want to. You know what it is like now to be helpless. I hope you'll remember it. And of course," he added, "we will all be back this way again next summer."

"Oh, golly, I guess we'll remember all right," said Jack. "We—I guess we didn't real-ize—"

"That's all I want to know," said Mr. Boom-schmidt. "And now, if anybody wants a ride on the elephant, step right up. Free rides for every-body."

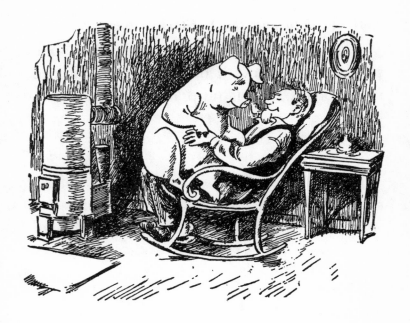

Chapter 17

It was late in the afternoon when Freddy and
the mice and the ducks finally got home. The
Beans had gone out for a drive, so all the farm
animals gathered in the cow barn, and Freddy
told them about their adventures. Uncle Wesley
was a good deal of bother, because he kept interrupting all the time to tell what *he* had thought
or what *he* had done. For since his parachute
jump, there had been no holding him. He
seemed to believe firmly that it had been his

idea to jump, and that Alice and Emma had jumped only because they had been shamed into it by his courageous example.

At last, after about the twentieth interruption, Freddy turned on him. "Look here, Uncle Wesley," he said. "If you're coming back to live on this farm, the time has come for you to hear some straight talk. We never used to call your bluffs, because Alice and Emma believed in you, and we didn't want to hurt them. But they know now that you aren't the hero you pretend to be."

"Well, well, well," said Uncle Wesley, swelling up angrily. "That sort of talk comes well from you, I must say. *You* didn't jump out of any balloon."

"No, but I wasn't pushed out by mice, either," said Freddy.

"Nonsense! Pushed out by mice indeed! I never heard—"

"All right," said Freddy. "We'll settle it right now. If you'll go up and jump out of the upper barn door, I won't say another word."

"I guess that's all you can do now, Wesley," said Mrs. Wiggins.

"Balderdash!" exclaimed the duck. "I refuse to be a party to any such ridiculous performance. Come, Alice—Emma! If these animals can't show a proper respect for my dignity and my standing in the community, I shall have to refuse to allow you to have anything to do with them. Come, we will go."

But Alice and Emma didn't move.

"Maybe you'd better jump, Uncle Wesley," said Emma after a moment. "Uncle Wesley isn't afraid," she said to Mrs. Wiggins. "He just feels that he doesn't want to be forced to do something that is beneath his dignity."

"Oh, my land!" said Mrs. Wiggins impatiently. "What does he think he is—a judge of the Supreme Court or something? I don't say anything against dignity, though land knows I never could manage to have much, but when somebody calls you a coward, is it undignified to prove he's wrong?"

Alice looked at Emma, and the two sisters turned and waddled up the stairs and disappeared in the loft above. A minute later the other animals, looking out through the doorway, saw them come sailing gracefully down through the air. Alice even turned a somersault before they landed in the barnyard. Then they came back into the barn.

There was a good deal of applause, but Uncle Wesley merely glared.

"The most undignified performance I ever hope to see," he said cuttingly. "I am really at a loss to account for the change in you two since I have been away. Goodness knows I spared no pains in your upbringing, and I felt that I could always count on you to be modest and ladylike in your behavior. But this—this tomboyish exhibition, and at your years—"

"Stop!" said Alice suddenly.

Uncle Wesley's bill dropped open and he stared at her in amazement. "You—you interrupted me!" he exclaimed.

"Yes, I did," replied Alice. "And I might as well tell you, Uncle Wesley, that we have indeed changed since you've been away. As long as we believed that you were as gallant and fearless as you said you were, we were willing to do as you said. But we have found you out. Perhaps, because you are our uncle, we might still be willing to be guided by you in all our actions.

. . . saw them come sailing gracefully down through the air.

But I think now we have our own dignity to consider. And so we have decided—Emma and I—that while we will be glad to have you come back and live with us again, in the future *you* will do as *we* say."

"To think," began Uncle Wesley, "that my own flesh and blood—"

"And," continued Alice, calmly interrupting him again, "we don't intend to argue about it. As our friend Jinx says—somewhat vulgarly, I am afraid, but it expresses our meaning—you'll take it and like it! Am I right, sister?"

"Oh, dear," said Emma nervously, "it seems terrible, but . . ." She hesitated, then drew herself up. "You said it, sister!" she exclaimed.

For Uncle Wesley this was the last blow. His head drooped, and he walked to the doorway and stood sadly looking out. Then suddenly he gave a start. "Dear me!" he said. "Why, goodness gracious!" He turned and looked oddly at his nieces. "Why, this is—this is . . ."

"Good grief, Wesley, what *is* it?" demanded Mrs. Wiggins.

"The duck stared at her with a sort of wondering look on his face. "I—I don't quite know how to tell you," he said. "It just came over me —why, I'm not a hero at all! And I don't care! Now that's a strange thing. All these years—" He broke off. "I have always admired heroism very much," he went on after a moment. "I didn't know I wasn't a hero myself. All those things I told you about my bravery—well, I thought they were true, or at least I thought they could be true. But now I see they couldn't. Dear me, I must be a coward! And what does it matter? Why, it relieves me of a tremendous strain, the strain of always having to act up to something I wasn't. I'm scared even of Alice and Emma—I've always been scared of them: that's why I bossed them around—so they wouldn't know it. But I'm getting too old for that. It's too much work." He turned to his nieces. "My dears," he said, "I would like to come back and live with you, if you want me. And I'll do as you say. Why, I think maybe I'll have a pretty good time!"

"That's the kind of talk I like to hear," said Mrs. Wiggins heartily. "I'm proud of you, Wesley." And the other animals crowded up and shook hands with him and patted him on the back.

"Why, you like me!" he exclaimed, and began to cry.

"Sure we like you," said Jinx, "now you're not a pompous old flutterbudget any more."

Freddy had heard the Beans drive into the yard some time ago, and now he picked up the two hundred dollars and went out to find Mr. Bean. The farmer was sitting on the front porch while Mrs. Bean could be heard clattering the dishes in the kitchen as she got supper. Freddy went up on the porch and put the packet of bills on the farmer's knee.

"Eh?" said Mr. Bean, looking at him sharply, and then he took up the bills and counted them. "By cracky!" he said. "By cracky!"

Mr. Bean never said "By cracky!" unless he was pretty deeply moved, and now he had said it twice. Freddy felt very happy, and he went up and rested his chin on Mr. Bean's knee.

A little while later Mrs. Bean went to the front parlor window and started to rap on it to call Mr. Bean in to supper. But what she saw stopped her. Mr. Bean, with his unlit pipe in his mouth, was rocking peacefully to and fro in the old willow rocker, and Freddy was sitting in his lap.

"Land sakes!" exclaimed Mrs. Bean. And then she laughed a little to herself, and went out and put Mr. Bean's supper on the back of the stove to keep it warm.

A NOTE ON THE TYPE

The text of this book was set on the Linotype in Baskerville. Linotype Baskerville is a facsimile cutting from type cast from the original matrices of a face designed by John Baskerville. The original face was the forerunner of the "modern" group of type faces.

John Baskerville (1706-75), of Birmingham, England, a writing-master, with a special renown for cutting inscriptions in stone, began experimenting about 1750 with punch-cutting and making typographical material. It was not until 1757 that he published his first work. His types, at first criticized, in time were recognized as both distinct and elegant, and his types as well as his printing were greatly admired.